They were playing a dangerous game.

"Maggie," he whispered in her ear. "The guy has a gun pointed at us and no one is watching now. We need to disappear before he regains his senses."

They both hit the door at a run. Just as daylight and cold city air blasted him in the face, the zing of a bullet whizzed past his ear and hit the front window. Glass shattered everywhere.

Bending, he threw his arm over Maggie's head and shuffled the two of them out the door as fast as he could. "Move!"

She took off without a word, but managed to keep up with him as he dashed along the packed sidewalks. They ran full-out and pushed through midday crowds until they were both out of breath.

"What the hell did you think you were doing?" he gritted out.

Maggie turned and gave him a sweet smile. "Why, Colin, darlin', you know the answer to that. I was saving your sorry life. What else?"

Dear Reader,

When I began THE SAFEKEEPERS trilogy, I thought of the three traits that I believed portrayed the best of womankind: courage, motherhood and love. The heroines in each of the three stories take a journey to becoming the best woman they can be—by living up to these traits. In this last book, I've embodied my ideals of the best of all three traits into one woman. For even though she may never have a child of her own, Maggie Ryan must find the courage to seek out trouble. She must accept both the joy and pain of mothering a child she may never be able to keep. And she must learn to give herself over to true love in order to become the best mother possible.

Maggie is one of my favorite heroines. She's tough enough to take what she needs. But she must also learn to be vulnerable enough to lose it all—in order to win the one thing she wants most! Count on Maggie to find a way. It's been great fun writing this trilogy. I hope you enjoy it as much as I did!

Happy Reading!

With all my best,

Linda

LINDA CONRAD

In Safe Hands

Silhouette®

Romantic

SUSPENSE

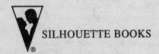

SILHOUETTE BOOKS

Recycling programs
for this product may
not exist in your area.

ISBN-13: 978-0-373-27628-8
ISBN-10:   0-373-27628-1

IN SAFE HANDS

Copyright © 2009 by Linda Lucas Sankpill

Visit Silhouette Books at www.eHarlequin.com

Printed in U.S.A.

LINDA CONRAD

was inspired by her mother, who gave her a deep love of storytelling. "Mom told me I was the best liar she ever knew. And that's saying something for a woman with an Irish storyteller's background!" Winner of many writing awards, including a *Romantic Times BOOKreviews* Reviewers' Choice Award and a Maggie Award, Linda often appears on bestseller lists. Her favorite pastime is finding true passion in life. Linda, her husband and KiKi the puppy, work, play, live and love in the sunshine of Florida.

To everyone who believes in magic.

Prologue

I curse you, Brody Ryan! May you and your children be forever barren. From this moment forward, no Ryan of your loins shall parent a child. No grandchild will you live to see! Your family name ends with your children, Brody Ryan, you son of a dog! Vete p'al carajo!

The *bruja*'s dark curse still rang out in Lupe Delgado's mind a decade and a half after it had been issued. More of a good witch, the *curandera* shook off the memory of her mother's harsh words from long ago. She continued her walk down the beach along a tropical Vera Cruz mountain lake, glancing again at the disturbing note that she had just been handed. Her mother, the ancient, black-magic *bruja* witch, was dying.

Lupe had known this time was coming. After all, her mother's lifetime stretched well into her nineties, and her health had been precarious lately. But Lupe wished with her whole heart for her mother to be granted more time. The fifteen-year-old curse was still valid, and her mother's shadowy soul was still unprepared to meet her God. Lupe's eyes filled with tears as her thoughts turned to her three Ryan grandchildren, who were currently living their adult lives in Texas. Their great-grandmother had cursed them when she cursed their father, and they had suffered from the old woman's black magic ever since. Lupe's mother's furious words had brought disaster down upon them, not to mention a blackened soul for the old woman herself.

After leaving the beach and returning home to her potions and crystals, Lupe packed up a small traveling kit. Her mother had finally relented a few months ago and renounced her black ways. The old woman was refusing to sell dark charms and hexes to her former customers. With her approaching death, Maria Elena Ixtepan had also agreed to reverse the curse on the Ryan children—*if* their father managed to perform three selfless deeds.

Lupe had not expected a miracle from her arrogant and defiant son-in-law, Brody Ryan. But so far he had accomplished two good deeds, and Lupe foresaw the possibility of complete redemption in the near future.

They were so close to salvation. Her mother just had to last a little longer.

With prayers in her heart, Lupe started out in the direction of her mother's mountainside cabin. She knew her own *curandera* white witchcraft abilities should not be used for such dubious purposes. But perhaps, if Lupe prayed to the right combination of saints and used the proper combination of words, she could keep death from her mother's doorstep long enough to save them all.

She had to try.

Chapter 1

Colin Fairfax took another shot of brandy from the flask he'd begun keeping in his pocket and resumed pacing the threadbare carpet in the rundown New York flat.

Bugger. It was freezing in here. No wonder the place was all but deserted. What kind of human could live for long in conditions like this? He'd agreed to wait for twenty-four hours, but now he was wondering if that had been the most intelligent thing to do.

He'd been through much worse, of course. Fighting alongside his men in freezing blizzards in the mountain passes in Afghanistan, he had known hell. Yet, even that extreme cold hadn't chilled his bones the same way the icy drafts singing down the tenement walls were battering both his body and his psyche.

He fingered the weapon at his waistband. Colin was pleased he'd thought of obtaining the automatic from his embassy before embarking on this personal mission. The secretive man he was supposed to meet claimed to have information that would be the most vital clue in Colin's search to date. According to other local contacts, this man was covertly employed by the Americans. His job was to keep tabs on just the sort of thing Colin wanted to find. Allowances had to be made for that kind of knowledge.

Covert was one thing, though. Being stupid was quite another.

Impatiently awaiting the creak of floorboards on the stairs outside his door, Colin wasn't sure how much longer he could bide his time in this godforsaken hovel. Once again he wondered why the man had been so insistent that they meet in this place and on this date.

But obtaining information about his brother, John, from the mystery man who called himself *"El Cuervo"* was important enough to keep Colin right here, freezing his bum for the duration.

A sudden soft knock from the other side of the door took Colin by surprise. At last. An end to this ridiculous waiting.

Blowing out a pent-up breath and deciding that his best defense was the element of surprise, he ripped open the flimsy wooden door, only to find a curly headed leprechaun standing in the shadows of the threshold.

"What?" he asked irritably and half turned away. This person resembled one of his annoying mother's fairie creatures. It couldn't be the man he'd been expecting.

"Colin?"

That word caught his attention, and he swung back. A low and sexy female voice had come from the short, lumpy body—and that voice had spoken his name.

Colin did what his gut told him to do. He grabbed her by the shoulders and lifted her off her feet as he popped her into the room. Using his foot, he slammed the door behind them. Then, reaching out with a steadying hand, he turned her around so that he could better study the small, odd female in the combined glow from an overhead bulb and the dusty lamp on his makeshift desk. Was she carrying a weapon?

"Hey!" she complained as she batted at his hands. "Cut out the manhandling." She sounded as surprised to be here as he'd been when she appeared at his door.

No gun. And at an inch or two over five feet tall, she posed no immediate danger.

"Who are you and what do you want?" he demanded.

She took off the mannish, gray fedora and a tumble of auburn curls spilled out over her shoulders and halfway down her back. Colin revised his original opinion. Not a leprechaun at all. No. Even in the shadowed glow of lamplight, the sight of this woman's wide and frightened eyes sent a sucker punch of heat straight to his gut. She was actually quite beautiful underneath the ugly green covering. But that doe-eyed look made her appear vulnerable—and too much like the very thing he'd long ago vowed to steer clear of. A lovely woman in distress. Trouble.

He needed to get his head in the game. She knew his name. Perhaps she had been sent with information. She seemed benign, if disconcerting, but she could turn out to be as potentially deadly as one of those beautiful, deserted passes belonging to mujahadin fighters in Afghanistan.

With his senses strung tight, Colin tried to ignore his primal response to her. He was certainly experienced enough to maintain appearances.

Except for her hair. Colin lost focus again, as he stared at that glorious hair. Even in the dim light he could see a hundred different colors shining throughout her mass of curls. Reds and chestnut and ebony. Even a few sprinkles of burnished gold. His hands ached to glide their way through that silken, shiny mane.

She stared at him, and the bare overhead bulb shot a single glimmer of light into her eyes. They were forest-green. The color was blinding.

Whoever the woman was, her body came in a riot of colors under the drab garments. Perhaps she truly was a leprechaun in disguise, sent to guard the pot of gold.

At that wayward thought, Colin took a sharp breath. Was John the pot of gold?

"Answer me, woman. What do you know?" Furiously he blinked away the guilt and pain that always came when he thought of John.

She simply stood there, eyes wide. A compulsive urge to lift a hand to her face and brush aside a flyaway strand of hair had Colin balling up his hands and gritting his teeth. He forced himself to step back and think clearly, reminding himself why he was here.

"My name is Maggie Ryan," she finally said with a lilting voice and an odd accent. "I've come a long way to seek you out. You hold the key to a child's future."

As the tall man gaped at her from out of those steely gray–blue eyes, Maggie tried to take in the whole picture with one quick glance, the way she'd trained herself to do. Age about midthirties. Clean-cut, with a strong chin. A touch of gray at his temples, and an expression that seemed both sharp and wary. Her initial impression was of a man both sophisticated and deadly. An odd combination.

But Maggie Ryan wasn't one to turn tail and run at the first sign of trouble. Even as a kid, she'd stood her ground against both her older brothers and against the magic forces in nature that swirled around their Texas family. She felt tough enough to get any job done. Especially one this important.

Absently, she fingered the protection charm that was tied to a leather thong around her neck, reminding herself of the alternate ways to defend herself, in lieu of wielding ordinary weapons. Her thoughts turned to her Mexican grandmother, Abuela Lupe, and all the lessons in witchcraft and magic she'd learned at her knee.

Maggie had also learned a few lessons in self-defense from her Irish-American private-investigator grandfather before he died, and those would serve her well. But right now she thanked goodness for Abuela Lupe. Her Mexican *curandera* grandmother had located this dangerous-looking man in her crystals and then told Maggie where and when to find him.

All that Maggie knew so far was that his name was Colin and he was the key to solving all of her problems.

He took her by the arm and dragged her closer. "I expect an explanation—*now*," he demanded in his clipped English accent. "What's all this nonsense?"

His touch sent heat scorching through her body. She couldn't remember a time that she'd had such a spontaneous, emotional response to a man. Well, not since the idiocy of an ill-advised engagement during her college years. If she'd had a mind to start *that* kind of thing again, this intense man, with his quiet British accent, his tailored slacks and expensive black leather jacket, would *not* be her choice of fiancé.

"Can we…um…sit down? To talk." Looking around, she found that the only chair had papers stacked on the seat.

He scooped up the papers and moved them to the bed. "Sit, then." Folding his hands behind his back in military style, Colin began to pace up and down the tiny room.

"What or who could be so important, Maggie Ryan," he said with an arrogant half smile, "that you sought me out through…a…" He shot his hand in the air as if lost for words. "What? How did you find me? A magic spell?"

He didn't know how close to the truth that was.

Maggie sat on the shaky chair with its one leg shorter than the others and stared up at him. "I've come all the way from south Texas to find answers about a lost child. It's the most important thing in the world. I'm trying to locate relatives for the orphaned baby girl in my custody. It's vital that—"

"Why me? Why come looking for me?"

Instead of answering she threw a question back at him. "You don't live in this room, do you? This can't be your home."

It was a good guess, since her grandmother had been so specific about her arriving at this place at just the right time. Besides, this man didn't look as if he belonged in a dump like this one.

She sucked up a breath and took a chance. "Why are you here?"

Colin's whole body seemed to jerk at her question. The smile disappeared and the dangerous man returned. She could see the change in those glacial eyes.

Bloody hell, Colin thought. *She knows something and she's just playing games.*

He swept closer, loomed over her, grabbed a handful of her hair. With a swift jerk, he tugged her head back, exposing the exquisite, smooth column of her neck.

"You haven't answered my question. Stop playing around. What do you know about my brother? Tell me quick, love, or I'll break that pretty neck of yours."

Maggie blinked. "Let go of my hair." She said it in a steady voice, though he could feel her trembling.

Without warning, a heated tingle traveled from her silky hair into his fingers and right up his arm. He released her involuntarily and rubbed his hands together to quiet the electric jolt he'd experienced.

"Your brother?" she asked, acting as if nothing happened when he released her. "I'm not sure. I mean… what's your brother's name?"

Outside the filthy window, winter storm clouds covered the moon. Colin's heart clouded over, too, with a gut instinct about what this eccentric beauty would say. For months now, he'd been feeling that the worst had happened. But he needed to hear the words.

"His name is John Fairfax," Colin managed to say in a strangled voice. "And if you know anything about his whereabouts, you had better speak up."

She looked thoughtful. "That could be it, I guess. The man's name was John. But the last name was Sheridan." She paused. "What's your full name?"

Suddenly furious with her for answering questions with more questions, he growled, "Sir Colin Fairfax, Baron Derwent. Also referred to recently as *Major* Colin Fairfax of the Third Royal Tank Regiment, Her Majesty's *British* Army, retired. Look, skip over any other questions that may pop into that lovely head of yours and get to the point. What do you know of John?"

Suddenly weary, Colin turned his back on her and began pacing again. She had used the past tense. He knew what that implied. His younger brother, the one he had lost track of several years ago due to his own misplaced arrogance and indifference, was very likely dead.

Maggie heard the hoarse but heartfelt words and began to experience Colin's growing misery herself, by way of empathic sympathy. "I have to start with the story of the baby."

Looking up into his bleak eyes as he strode by, she wished she wasn't so sure about the facts. "That's how I got involved in the first place. I live near the border, and about six months ago a couple and their two-month-old daughter were involved in a terrible car crash on our side of the river. The couple died on impact, but the baby in the backseat survived."

Sighing, she continued. "The sheriff asked me to take the child into my home, as our isolated county doesn't have any local child welfare services. My neighbor, who runs a day-care center, helps me out when needed." Maggie swallowed hard, wishing she could be wrong but knowing full well she wasn't, and went on. "I'm a trained private investigator, so I've been looking into the deceased's backgrounds ever since I took in the child, trying to trace any relatives of the little girl."

A perplexed expression crossed Colin's face as he quit pacing and slowly shook his head. "I don't understand. Are you saying my brother married? Fathered a child? Impossible. I would've known."

"How long has it been since you've seen him?"

Maggie asked, going on instinct. "Why are you search-ing for information about your own brother?"

Even in the dim lighting of the sordid room, Maggie could clearly see the pain streak through Colin's eyes. She hurt for him. If it had been one of her brothers…

Nevertheless, she was still wary. When Colin accepted the facts, would he be willing to leave Emma in her care? Or would he do the unthinkable and demand she hand over his niece? Maggie's life would stop if that happened. She needed this child. Emma had become her heart—her only chance. With cold fear trickling through her at the possibilities, Maggie reminded herself to take things slow and not jump ahead.

"I…uh…" Colin looked around, staring absently at his surroundings as if he'd only just arrived. "Our family was divided when John and I were children, ages ten and twelve, respectively. As the eldest, I stayed in my father's care, went to his old school and joined his regiment in due course. John went with our mother to her family's ancestral home in Ireland." The words, sounding as if they were spoken by rote, seemed to grow small in Colin's throat. "As long as my father was alive, we con-tinued to receive word of my brother's welfare."

Maggie's icy, worried feelings began to melt, as warm tears welled in her eyes. "Your father died recently?"

"It's been several years since he passed away," Colin answered with a bleak expression. "But I only returned to civilian life four months ago, after a long tour of duty, and then began looking for my brother."

Maggie waited. There was a lot more to tell, she was sure. But she wasn't sure how much of it Colin would be willing to give up to a complete stranger.

Funny, though, sometime in the last few minutes

she'd stopped thinking of him as a stranger who could take away her whole world. Something about him called to her. Disturbed her, yes, yet made him appear much more like a friend in stranger's clothing.

Still, she hoped he wouldn't touch her again. The last two times had completely thrown her out of balance with shots of sexual energy the likes of which she hadn't known existed.

A few moments of silence had apparently given Colin a chance to regain some self-control. He stopped pacing and turned to her. "Why are you asking questions? Weren't you sent to talk to me by *El Cuervo?*"

"The Raven?" Maggie let the English translation roll off her tongue, but a chill ran down her spine. "No one sent me. I sought you out because—"

She sensed the danger an instant before catching sight of a flash of color outside the window.

"Watch out!" Maggie jumped up, knocking hard into Colin's side at the exact moment the window exploded. Shattered glass and bits of broken wood frame sprayed everywhere as the two of them hit the floor.

Surprised but unhurt, and by no means out of commission, Colin rolled Maggie under him for protection and reached for the SIG Sauer at his back. A loud bang was quickly followed by a hail of bullets through the window. He ducked his head, and when he looked around, fire had ignited in a corner of the room. *Bugger it*.

From beneath his body, he heard Maggie mumbling what sounded like a chant, but the words weren't in English. They weren't in Gaelic, either, which could've been expected from her name. They sounded for all the world like a unique kind of Spanish.

The idea of her speaking Spanish made him wonder

if she might be part of the Mexican drug lord's conspiracy. It could be that she was lying about everything just to set him up. Did she know more than she'd said? Especially concerning the international drug sting that had sent John into hiding in the first place?

Ignoring his suspicions for the moment, Colin tensed further at the sudden, deadly quiet and got to his feet. He stayed hunched over as he palmed his weapon and flattened his body against the wall between the door and the window. He took aim out the window, trying to get a fix on the shadowy fire escape of the opposite building—without making himself too great a target.

He gave Maggie a swift glance. If she was guilty, then her own cohorts had turned against her. But Maggie Ryan could not be left to die in a burning room. It was unthinkable, despite the fact she could have betrayed him. It would be up to him to fight their way out.

"Colin, move farther away from the door. Hurry!"

Maggie crawled closer and jerked at his hand, trying to pull him down. He twisted from her grip and concentrated on targeting anything that moved outside the window. From the corner of his eye, he saw Maggie grab again at his pant's leg, finally giving it one gigantic tug.

Off balance now, he heard another blast just as the wall at his side burst apart. By then it was far too late to move out of the way.

Everything faded to black.

Chapter 2

Maggie dragged a woozy Colin and his duffel down the shadowed sidewalk. Good thing darkness still reigned in the wee small hours here in the valley between skyscraper mountains. Not many people were out in the crisp night air, though quite a lot of cars still filled the streets. A big red bus stopped at the corner of the block, belching smelly exhaust. The few people who'd been waiting began to board.

She'd considered taking the subway back to her hotel, but had dismissed the idea when she thought about Colin negotiating all those station steps. He seemed delirious, and she wasn't positive he knew what was going on. He could barely walk. His wound wasn't bleeding anymore, but if he was in shock, there was nothing she could do for him until they returned to her room. A taxi would be simple, of course, but they were scarce here and she didn't want to deal with a curious driver.

Hailing the bus driver to wait, she climbed the bus steps, pulled Colin along with her and found two empty seats. During the fifteen-minute ride neither of them spoke a word. Colin closed his eyes and rested.

She felt his body heat without even touching him. Colin's nearness did crazy things to her, in both body and mind, but she couldn't get past the dangerous position he'd put them in. Who on earth was this guy really, and who wanted to kill him?

At long last she spotted the side street that led to her hotel's entrance and hurried them off the bus. The hotel that she'd checked into earlier couldn't be called a palace, but it was sure a heck of a lot better than Colin's flophouse room.

Small by Texas standards, the room was at least clean and warm. And temporarily safe. She snuck Colin past the reception desk and into the elevator. When Maggie finally keyed open her door and tumbled Colin and herself inside, she was so danged relieved that she nearly cried.

Her witchcraft would help heal Colin. The sooner he was pain free, the sooner they could talk, and then she'd be that much closer to leaving New York City and Colin's trouble far behind her.

Plopping him down on the single bed, she shoved pillows behind his back and helped him kick off his shoes. "You rest while I check your leg."

She turned, but his hand snaked out and grabbed her arm. "You're not leaving."

"No, of course not. That's not what I said." Swinging back to reassure him, she caught the look he'd been giving her behind her back. Wary. Stark. Lonely. The stricken look on his face struck a deep note of sympathy in her heart.

"You'll not be calling your friends, love?"

"What friends?" She pulled her arm from his grasp then placed her palm against his forehead, checking for fever.

"The ones who must have come with you. The chaps with the fire bombs and guns."

He thought *she* was the one who'd brought that disaster down upon them? "I might ask you the same question," she said, realizing he had a small fever but nothing her medicine couldn't cure. "All I did was come to bring you news of your brother and niece, and I got shot at and nearly burned to death for my trouble. I was hoping you would have the answers as to why."

Colin groaned and grabbed his thigh. "Don't leave, Maggie." He closed his eyes, slumped back against the pillows and was fast asleep in an instant.

Swell. Now she was faced with checking his wounds without his assistance. Determined to do the best she could for the man who had caused her even more inner turmoil than whoever'd been doing the shooting, she went to the closet to retrieve her medicine pack.

Maggie Ryan was tough. She could do anything. Isn't that what everybody always said?

Being tough was one of the traits that had turned her only boyfriend—her college fiancé—against her. In a fit of anger over losing what he'd thought would be his meal ticket for life, he pushed it even further, accusing her of being frigid and asking for his ring back.

That was the last time she'd let a man get close to her. But she was feeling things for Colin that she'd never felt for her ex-fiancé.

Too close. She was too close to caring for this complete stranger. She needed to remind herself why she'd sought him out on this dark and icy night in the first place.

When Colin opened his eyes, it took him a moment to orient himself. He felt beneath his body and discovered he was lying on some sort of bed or mattress. But with the jumbled thoughts in his head, nothing else seemed clear.

The pain in his thigh was most definite, though, and sharp enough to make him more alert. The memory of the wall exploding behind him kept repeating, and the sound of Maggie Ryan's voice begging him to get down echoed clear and true in his ears.

Was he still in danger? Probably not. Because wherever he was, everything seemed absurdly quiet after all the commotion. Colin's survival instincts lay still. Nothing screamed in his gut to either run or fight.

Turning his head, he pried open his eyes and glanced around. He found himself in some sort of bland and inexpensive hotel room. He'd seen many of these same small rooms around the world.

"You're awake again. Good. Do you think you can sit up?"

It was *her* voice. Maggie's. That same smoky pitch he remembered from when she'd appeared at his doorway.

Colin tried to rise, but he had little strength in his arms and one hell of a pain in his leg. "Where am I?"

Her soft, feminine arms slid under his back, and with a surprising show of strength, Maggie lifted him to a sitting position. "There you go. You're in my hotel room. Does it hurt very much?"

Clearing the fog from his head, Colin stared once again at the most striking-looking woman he had ever beheld. The fantastic mass of curls he remembered from before as being dark auburn looked the color of burnt cinnamon in this light. The ugly, pea-colored coat was gone. She wore a long-sleeved, western-cut shirt with blue and red stripes, tucked into dark-blue jeans.

He focused on her face, his gaze skimming across clear golden skin and a soft, full mouth. But it was the eyes that drew him in. Still startling. Still the vivid green of an Irish mist. Just looking at them produced a surprising and unwelcome reaction in his groin.

"I have a few questions for you."

She had questions? Since Colin's brain had begun working past the pain, a million blasted questions sat unasked on his tongue.

"But I need to finish working on your leg first," she added.

"How did I get here?" He couldn't let her get ahead of him. His control was shaky, but he didn't trust her enough to close his eyes again.

"You and I sort of limped over here on the bus, after we got out of that room one step ahead of the fire-fighter first responders. You were a little shocked and dizzy, but we made it."

He gave her a disbelieving look, but she seemed undeterred.

"The shot that hit you only nicked the fleshy part of your thigh. No bullet fragments were left behind, I checked. You've got a couple of cuts on your forehead, but none of them are deep." She paused. "I was afraid to stick around and wait for the cops or the paramedics. Someone must want you dead pretty badly."

"Yes, it does seem that way." But was she in on it? He'd been waiting in that room all day, and the shooting had started only after she'd arrived. "Never mind. Where are my pants, love?"

"I had to cut them off you to get to the wound. But you packed another pair. I brought your duffel with us as I dragged you out of the fire. Thankfully, your leather jacket was only singed in a few spots, but it should be—"

"*You* dragged me out of the room? By yourself?"

She gave him a sharp smirk before turning her back to dig into his duffel. "I'm tougher than I look."

Yeah, he would bet she was quite a lot of things underneath those exotic looks. Grace, strength and a sort of magical beauty must have been bestowed upon her at birth by the fairies. But something sinister seemed to lurk about her as well.

He'd already made up his mind to find out everything. She would tell him first whether she had been sent to do him harm, and then she would complete her tale about his brother. The truth. Every bit of it.

It mattered little that her appearance affected him like no other woman's. With everything they'd been through, he couldn't imagine why his body kept betraying him with primal, sexual reactions. But he swore to set all that aside.

"What are you up to, Maggie Ryan? How did you know where to find me?"

Maggie winced inwardly, not sure how to explain. "I'll tell you everything as best I can. But let me work on your leg at the same time."

He didn't bat an eyelash, just continued staring her down.

"Please. I swear I can help you. Let me."

Something must have gotten to him, either her words or the way she stood up to him, because he relented at last. "What are you planning then? Shall we cut off the blasted leg entirely?"

The words had been said without so much as a smile, but they made her chuckle. "Heavens no. I have some…um…lotions that I'll make into a poultice. It'll relieve the pain, I promise. And I can put a couple of sutures in, too, if need be."

Maggie bent to paw through the denim backpack containing her medicines. "Can you lie back again, please?"

She took her bag into the bathroom and mixed up her healing concoctions. Back at his side, Maggie went straight to work, splashing *blanquillo*, a clear liquid, over his leg.

Ready now to apply the poultice she'd made, Maggie gazed into his eyes. "This shouldn't hurt. Try not to move."

He stopped her by holding up his hand. "Tell me what's in the poultice first."

Impatiently, Maggie shook her head. "Look, I have training as a *curandera*—a healer—in Texas and Mexico. I can take away your suffering."

When he continued to stare at her, she sighed and went on, "The poultice contains herbs and dried plants, nothing harmful. Let me—"

"Which herbs and plants?"

Gritting her teeth, she told him. "It's a basic mixture of basil, rosemary and rue, the holy trinity for Mexican witchcraft." When he didn't flinch at the word *witchcraft*, she went on. "To those I've added three specially dried plants. Mexican arnica—"

"Camphor weed. Yes, I can smell the astringent. What else?"

Surprised, she went on. "Spikenard for open sores and silk tassel for the pain reliever."

"I recognize the name silk tassel, it's called quinine bush in some places. But the other…"

"It's rare. Also called elk clover, and found only in a few mountain areas in the Southwestern United States and Mexico."

He nodded his head and lay back against the pillows. "Okay, go ahead. But I want your story at the same time. I'd wager you're the kind of witch that can do at least two things at one time."

"How do you know so much about the healing properties of some pretty obscure plants?"

With his eyes closed, he answered in a weak voice, "I've spent time in some pretty obscure places in the world. The uses for medicinal plants and herbs are not just the province of Mexican witches, you know."

His eyes flickered open again for a brief moment. "But quit hedging, woman. Begin your story."

She began applying the poultice. "I'm from a little town in south Texas near the Mexican border. A place called Zavala Springs. It's a ranching town, surrounded by the multithousand-acre Delgado Ranch. You may have heard of the ranch, it's pretty famous. The Delgado Ranch is my family's heritage, but the whole area is a really nice place to live and grow up in."

Was that a good enough recommendation to entice him to leave Emma there? Probably not.

Colin sat back, watching her work with icy-blue eyes that were becoming evermore sharp and clear.

She decided to approach this from another direction.

"I'm really sorry to have to tell you this, but I'm sure your brother was the one killed in the auto accident late last spring. He was using the name John Sheridan and he and his wife had been living in Alexandria, Virginia."

Shaking his head, Colin leaned forward and spoke with quiet danger in his voice. "In the first place, my brother wasn't married, as I said before. And second, how could you possibly connect a man named John Sheridan to my brother and then to me?" Not waiting for an answer, he plowed ahead. "I owe you a huge thanks for getting me out of that room, Maggie, and I'm grateful for your efforts at natural healing on my behalf. But what's the truth of why you sought me out? What aren't you telling me?"

She fought to get control of the conversation. "Look, I'm sure of my facts. You've been searching for your brother, haven't you? Why don't you tell me what you've learned already, and than we can compare what we know. I think what I know will hold up to whatever you have."

Colin had to admit that she'd saved his life. And if she had actually wanted him dead, there'd been plenty of opportunities to do the deed. But it was the vulnerable look in her eyes that finally got him this time.

What did he have to lose? "All right. Fine." He winced as she dabbed the poultice on his open wound. "I've discovered my brother was recruited by SIS, the British Secret Intelligence Service, while I was overseas at war."

That idea still troubled Colin. Had John gone into covert work in an effort to impress him? Perhaps to get his attention?

Focusing on the present, he went on, "A couple of years ago John participated in an international, interagency sting in Mexico. The mission was to infiltrate the Mexican drug trade, one organization in particular. But then the sting went sour and John disappeared."

Colin caught his breath and watched Maggie's expression as he finished the story. "It's taken me months to get a line on what happened to him, to assure myself that he wasn't murdered in Mexico. A contact in your state department let me know that John had been threatened, yes, but he'd escaped. Someone, a shadowy figure and difficult to find, knew of his whereabouts. That was the man I expected to meet, when you arrived instead—and the shooting started."

Maggie's eyes went wide. "I came only because I needed to ask how you feel about…"

Halting her stumbling words, Maggie worried that she'd already said too much in the wrong way, so she began again. "After we…um…buried the Sheridans and I took in their child, I made every attempt to locate relatives, however distant. I searched the Internet for months. Even the rental car agency records were of little help. I found out that the Sheridans had rented a townhouse in Alexandria about a year ago, but their neighbors don't remember much about them."

"Go on," he urged impatiently, while she gulped in a breath.

"Their licenses and the baby's birth certificate were registered there, but that seems to be where the trail begins and ends. It's like they appeared out of thin air a year ago." She sighed heavily. "So, while I was searching, I became their child's foster mother. Your niece's foster mother. How would you feel about…I mean…"

Her words died in her throat. She was too scared to ask.

"You still haven't said how you connected…"

"You to John Sheridan?" She refused to think of the consequences and plowed ahead. "Witchcraft. My Abuela Lupe helped me. She possesses crystals that *see* things hidden to others, and she knows how to use their special powers. We weren't looking for people so much as a specific location of the nearest relative."

Forcing herself to make eye contact, she continued, "That's how I knew where to find you. I'm sorry to be the bearer of such sad news."

Colin lifted the corners of his mouth in what could be either the ghost of a smile or a grimace. "Say for the moment that I…uh…buy into your witchcraft and crystal story, I still don't understand why a woman who appears—" he waved his hand at her "—as reasonable as you let herself be persuaded to come all this way based on crystals."

"I believe in my grandmother's magic absolutely. Besides that, now that I've seen you, I'm totally convinced you're the baby's uncle."

"Why?"

"You both have a very distinctive eye color. That clear ice-blue is not something I've seen before."

Colin looked uncomfortable about more than just the bandage she'd applied. "So I've been told. But it's not enough to assure me the child and I are related by blood. I wish for your sake it was."

This was getting them nowhere. Exhaustion was overtaking them both, making compromise—or even clear thought—impossible.

"Sleep for now," she whispered. "We'll talk about it more when you're rested. I won't let any harm come to you. Trust me."

"I don't trust easily, Maggie," Colin said as he lay

back. "But I will sleep. Then when I awake, we'll have the rest of our questions asked and answered. Count on it."

Sunlight streamed down the air shaft outside the hotel room window. Maggie had no idea how long she'd been asleep. Last night, she'd curled up in the overstuffed, ugly, flower-print chair, watching over a sleeping Colin until her eyelids grew too heavy to prop open.

She cast a sleepy glance toward the mussed-up bed and sat up. She couldn't believe her eyes. Colin was gone.

Holy moly. He must have slipped out while she was asleep. But why? She was fairly sure that she'd cured his wounds, but they hadn't finished talking about his brother—and more important to her, about the baby.

Jumping up, she checked the room. Colin's things were missing, too. *Darn.* She couldn't just leave and go home to Emma. Colin knew where she lived. He could show up on her doorstep any day and demand she turn over his niece.

Maggie knew what she needed to do. She had to find him. Had to make him agree—in writing—to leave the baby with her for good. She went to her pack and pulled out her grandmother's crystal, the one that could locate people.

She'd never tried this by herself before. Had never needed to. But this time, as she peered into the glass and focused her mind on finding Colin, the murky depths of the crystal began to clear and images began to form.

A shaft of panic slowly rose up through her spine as she saw Colin's silhouette in a back booth of a darkened bar. His eyes were trained toward the front door as if he were waiting for someone.

But then another vision came into view in the crystal. A man, hunched into a trench coat, approached the restaurant's back door. He slid his hand down into the coat pocket and withdrew a gun.

No!

Maggie grabbed her backpack and raced out the door and down the hotel's stairs. Her mind knew the way to go, and it was clear she had to go *now*.

But would she be in time to save his life?

Chapter 3

From his booth in the darkest corner of the bar, Colin watched while the blighter who'd dropped off his pint backed away from the table, muttering something in Spanish. Colin tried to ignore the twit's stares. He knew the fresh scratches on his face must look strange, but they'd already closed over with scabs and were healing thanks to Maggie's natural potions. Not much else he could do about them now.

Needing to test his muscles, he stretched in his seat. A little soreness remained, but none of the intense pain from before. That Maggie Ryan had done an amazing job on him.

He had no trouble understanding why he'd so easily accepted her natural healing ability, yet still could not believe her witchcraft story. Years earlier, he himself had received training from a *curandera* healer. His father had been a diplomat, stationed in the Mexican state of Vera Cruz at the time, and Colin went for summer holiday. He'd spent a couple of fascinating months there learning about natural healing, honing the healing skills he'd picked up years earlier from his Irish mother and grandmother.

Colin seldom allowed himself to dwell on his early lessons in native plants, or on the Irish half of his background for that matter. Such thoughts usually turned dark when they led to the uncomfortable memories of his mother's abandonment, and from there to thoughts of John, and the worthless reasons he'd given himself for neglecting his own brother.

He now knew that no amount of anger toward his mother was adequate grounds for deserting his baby brother. It hadn't been John's fault that their mother drove a wedge between the family. Colin realized, too late, that John had looked up to him, counted on him. And Colin had let him down. Stayed away when John needed his big brother the most.

Feeling melancholy, Colin tried to shake off the memories. He'd left Maggie's room because, if he'd stayed, he might have begun to believe all her stories. Her spirit had called to him, her body set his afire at first sight. He couldn't think clearly around her.

Natural healing was one thing, but witchcraft and crystals were quite another. Deep in his being, he did not believe.

He wasn't ready to give up on John. To admit he'd lost his only brother. Not yet.

After making a couple of phone calls, Colin had gotten hold of a man who swore to know the truth. He was to meet that man here, in this pub, in the middle of the day.

It now seemed a waste of time.

Without warning, Colin felt the cold steel of a gun barrel as it pressed against his neck.

"Don't move, Fairfax," the deep voice said in heavily accented English. "And don't make a sound."

Where had the bastard come from? Colin had been watching the front door, and the bloke had appeared out of nowhere.

"We're going to take this out to the alley. But if you make any wrong moves, I'd just as soon shoot you here. Understood?"

Colin nodded. His mind was busy calculating his chances, and the choice between making a stand here or out in the alley. Would this man have any real answers for him? Or was he just there to stop Colin's questions for good?

"Get up. Slowly, *por favor.*"

Colin found himself leaning more toward the idea that this *hombre* wanted to kill him, not talk. The thought chilled him to the bone. His brother must be dead after all.

Numb and heartsick, Colin shifted and slid out of the booth. The man at his side grabbed his arm and jammed the gun in his ribs.

"Now walk. Nice and easy, *sí?*"

A commotion in the front of the bar caught everyone's attention. Colin and his captor slowed then stopped dead.

"Colin, darlin'." A high-pitched female voice lilted through the barroom. "Don't you dare walk away from me, you…you… I've got something to say to you."

Colin turned and blinked at the sight of Maggie shoving her way through the tables and heading directly for him. She looked like an avenging angel, storming through the bar patrons, who all watched her every move. An angel in a familiar, pea-green coat. He wanted to warn her to stay away but hesitated to make any quick moves. Instead, he waited for a chance to take control of the situation. Colin knew he could wrestle the gun away from the smaller man at his side if all things were equal, but he didn't want anyone else to get hurt.

Particularly not Maggie.

She stormed up and raised her voice so she could be heard throughout the bar. "Colin Fairfax, you come home with me right this minute. How dare you leave just when I was telling you about the baby."

"What?"

Maggie grimaced and shoved at his chest. "Come on. Stand up like a man. Let's go home and face the music together." She grabbed his arm and tugged him away from the stunned gunman.

Colin shot a glance at the guy and saw the man's mouth had dropped open. Colin knew exactly how he felt. What the hell kind of game was she playing?

A dangerous one.

Maggie pulled him toward the front door. Every eye in the place was locked on the two of them.

"Maggie," he whispered in her ear. "The guy has a gun pointed at us and no one is watching him now. We need to disappear before he figures it out."

They both hit the door at a run. Maggie leaned against it and shoved. Just as daylight and cold city air blasted him in the face, the zing of a bullet whizzed past his ear and hit the front window. Glass shattered everywhere.

Bending, he threw his arm over Maggie's head and

shuffled the two of them out the door as fast as he could. "Move!"

As they hit the sidewalk, he took control and grabbed her arm. "Let's go. Run."

She started off without a word, managing to keep up with him as he dashed along the packed sidewalk. They ran full out and pushed through midday crowds until they were both out of breath.

Panting, he slowed after they'd gone about five blocks. "What the hell did you think you were doing?" he gritted out.

Maggie turned and gave him a sweet smile. "Why, Colin darlin', you know the answer to that. I was saving your idiotic ass. What else?"

The head of the notorious drug cartel leaned back in his cushioned chair and looked around the veranda. The men in his employ either ate, drank or played cards as they lay around and waited to do his bidding.

All his money. The power he had accumulated. It would all mean nothing if the one man with more power learned of his past foolish mistake. In fact, his whole life would be worthless.

Ten years it had taken. He had worked hard and smart enough to climb to the top of one of the largest Mexican drug cartels. It would be too humiliating to have it come down around his ears, all because he had needed to take one small bit of revenge.

In truth, he'd managed to become the *jefe*—the boss—by demanding respect, and everyone knew that respect must be maintained.

No one blamed him because his organization had been infiltrated by an international undercover operation. Those agents had had their jobs to do, and he had his. All is fair in such wars. In fact, when he'd learned of their operation—fortunately before much damage could be done to his own organization—he felt respect for the men who had planned such a daring sting.

Respect for everyone but the traitor who'd become his lieutenant. Sighing, he thought once again of Juan. Juan, who'd been like a son to him. Better even than his own sons, because the man had had polish. Juan had accomplished things that his sons and nephews could not. It had been Juan who negotiated the money exchanges with higher-ups, Juan who bought and sold the real properties, Juan who could talk to the *patrones* and the politicians with more culture and power. Without Juan, the *jefe's* connection with the big boss, Governor Garcia, would never have happened. His cartel would've been much less powerful.

Congenial and smart, Juan had been a tremendous help. The very idea that he'd been a spy all that time still rankled.

"*Jefe,* the *hombre* you wait for, was that him on the phone? *El Cuervo de la Muerte?* The Raven of Death?" Carlos, one of his men, had sucked up enough courage to interrupt the boss's thoughts.

He nodded. "Yes, but *El Cuervo* will find his own time on earth growing short. He has failed in his mission. I have issued orders."

"*El Cuervo* did not kill the Anglo? The nosy one?"

The *jefe* could swear he'd gone over these plans with Carlos earlier. Why couldn't the man remember even the most important things? Carlos's incompetence made him think of Juan, and that made him angry again.

"The Raven was supposed to eliminate Colin

Fairfax, Juan's brother. I cannot allow this Fairfax to continue asking questions. He must die. But *El Cuervo* missed his opportunity." The *jefe* spat out the words in a fury. "Twice. The Raven of Death will not live to fail a third time. There are others who can be bought who will not fail."

Carlos backed up and visibly shivered in his boots. "I do not understand the importance of this Fairfax. Juan is *muerto*. Why do you care if his brother asks questions? All the world should know *el jefe* demands respect and loyalty. The punishment for betrayal must be death." Carlos shrugged, as though the idea was obvious.

The *jefe* waved his underling away as he had no wish to continue this conversation. The truth was bad enough. He could not afford word of it to spread.

The mistake had not been his fault. How was he to know that the traitor, Juan, had married since he'd disappeared into hiding? No one had heard from Juan for nearly a year when the *jefe's* people finally managed to bribe a man who knew of his whereabouts. The minute he had been found, Juan's fate had been sealed, though the *jefe* paid extra to make it look like an accident.

Qué carajo! How was he to know about a marriage that had been kept a secret from everyone? The *jefe* groaned under his breath as he faced his bad luck. Even the killing of an innocent woman should not have been too terrible as collateral damage. Innocent people died in cartel slayings every day.

But it had turned out this woman was special. Of all the people on earth for Juan to have married and died beside, why had he chosen Governor Garcia's young daughter? And why had she chosen Juan as a means to escape her father?

Thankfully, the young couple had kept their romance quiet. It wasn't much of a break, but the *jefe* could use it. Governor Garcia was still looking for his missing daughter and had no idea she'd married. But the powerful man would find out eventually. And then he would not give up until he learned the rest. The governor didn't have his own black *brujo* magic the way the *jefe* did. He couldn't see the future in the crystals, nor frighten his enemies with hexes and curses, but the governor did have many of his own contacts, and much power. That made it imperative for the *jefe* to stop nosy questions before the wind could carry the news back to the governor's ears. All people asking those kinds of questions must disappear.

The *jefe's* hands shook as he tried to pour himself a drink. He had also just learned of something else that had the potential to be much worse news for him. Something he had somehow missed months ago and now wasn't sure he knew how to handle.

It seemed Juan and the governor's daughter had had a child together. A baby. And that baby lived, despite the "accident" that killed its parents.

Taking a much-needed shot of tequila straight and warm, the way it was meant to be, the *jefe* felt the familiar burn clear to his gut as he wondered what he should do about the child when he found it. And he would find it. It was only a matter of time.

"What were you thinking?" Maggie shoved at Colin's chest and narrowed her eyes at him. She should be giving him the evil eye, but he refused to look at her directly.

They'd quit running long enough to stop at the hotel, so Colin could pick up his duffel from the luggage check. Now they were down in Penn Station, trying to stay lost in the crowds. Colin kept his eyes shuttered from her view. She figured that meant he felt guilty for getting them both into that jam back at the bar. Well, he should. That was twice she'd had to save his life.

"Answer me. What the devil possessed you to try meeting with that man again? Are you crazy? Isn't one attempt on your life enough?"

He folded his arms over his chest, lifted his chin and gave her a cold appraisal. "I couldn't believe…the man I contacted is an agent for your government. I didn't expect anyone working for the United States to send an assassin. Rather cheeky of him, if you ask me. I was only trying to find the truth about my brother."

This wasn't a joke, darn it. Fuming, she grimaced as she stared him down. His nearness gave her goose bumps, but she wouldn't put up with any nonsense. She opened her mouth to tell him off, then promptly shut it again. Maggie couldn't be too hard on him. Not when she understood how devastated he must feel underneath everything else.

Besides, someone wanted him dead. That whole, wild idea made her knees weak.

"Let's sit a minute and settle down," she whispered.

They found a quiet alcove, and by some miracle, two empty seats. As Colin plopped both his duffel and himself down, he gave her a quick glance, then began studying his shoes. She could feel the silent grief rolling off him in waves. So he hadn't trusted her. Big deal. If she'd been in his place, she probably would've done the same.

Compassion colored her thoughts, making her heart go all mushy for the poor guy. She decided to give him a break—find a way to keep his mind off of dealing with the guilt.

By talking his ear off. "I have two brothers of my own, you know."

He shot her a questioning look, and she figured she was on the right track. Give him something else to think about.

"Oh yeah," she rambled on. "Two *big* brothers. When we were kids, it was both a blessing and a pain to have them hovering over me all the time. They taught me to ride and rope and swim. The three of us are real products of our environment. Have you ever been to south Texas?"

Without waiting for him to answer—without even taking a second breath—she babbled on. "After being separated for almost fifteen years, all of us are finally living within a few miles of each other. My oldest brother, Josh, he was a Ranger in the army. In Afghanistan. Did you say you were stationed in Afghanistan? You two might have met there.

"Anyway, my other brother, Ethan, was in the Secret Service, guarding big shots like ambassadors, and even the President of the United States on occasion. Both Josh and Ethan are back home in Texas now, helping me with my new business." Her voice softened. "Josh is married and Ethan is engaged. Both of them are in the process of adopting the kids that came along with the wonderful women in their lives. But that's another long story. I don't think you want to—"

Colin lifted his head and raised a hand. "Take a breath before you faint, love."

Maggie elbowed him in the ribs. She drew in a deep breath and tried to calm down, but kept her eyes trained on Colin's face. His expression seemed lighter, less sad.

"What kind of accent do you have?" he asked. "I've

been to a lot of places in the world, but I've never heard anything quite like it."

The idea hit her without warning. He needed to come home with her. Get out of this city and away from whatever danger stalked him. Colin should also take the opportunity to see his brother's grave and meet his darling baby niece. Maybe if he did all that, it would make him feel a little less guilty about losing track of his brother, give him closure of a sort.

And maybe…Well, if he saw that Emma was happy and healthy and living with people who adored her, maybe he would be more amenable to letting the baby stay where she was.

"The accent's a mishmash, same as me," she answered airily. "My granddaddy and Nana Ryan came over from Ireland as a young couple and never lost their Gaelic lilts. I probably picked up a little of their accent when I lived with them."

She sighed and drew in air. "And my Abuela Lupe, my mom's mother, speaks with a heavy Spanish accent. She's living in Mexico now, but she lived with us at the ranch until my mom died when I was fifteen. I learned a lot from her, including how to speak Spanish."

She had his full attention now. He was staring at her as if he was seeing her for the first time.

"Look," she began as she rose to her feet. "Why don't you fly home with me today? You can meet the baby and my family and friends. See your brother's grave."

He flinched at the mention of his brother.

With unexpected tears filling her eyes, she had to force herself to continue. "Maybe you'd like to put another headstone on his grave. One with the right name and all." Lordy, but she sure hoped he wouldn't want to take his brother's body back to England. She wanted baby Emma to be able to visit her daddy's grave when she got old enough to understand.

"Come to Texas with you?" Colin looked a little overwhelmed. But soon enough his eyes cleared and he too stood. "That's a brilliant idea, Maggie, love."

"Well…great. Let's go then." She turned, but kept right on talking over her shoulder as she picked up her backpack. "We can take the Air Train from here. It'll get us to the airport in enough time for—"

Colin grabbed her arm, swung her around and pulled her close. Too close. It took her breath away.

"Thank you for saving my life," he whispered against her lips as he gazed into her eyes. "I'm not sure how you managed all of this yet, but I owe you a debt."

"Uh. No." She could barely think while standing this close to the blue and silver highlights in his eyes. "You—"

Breaching the gap between them, he stopped her words—her thoughts, her breathing—by lasering a kiss across her lips. A sudden rush of fire through her veins turned her world upside down, and the unflappable Maggie Ryan finally hit the wall.

Chapter 4

That one blasted kiss! Whenever Colin had looked toward Maggie since their encounter, he'd found her still fingering her bottom lip. Even now, hours later, as she drove the four-wheel drive away from the San Antonio airport and headed toward her home in South Texas, her left hand absently touched her soft, full mouth. It was as if she couldn't quite get past the kiss they'd shared.

Well, hell, he was having a lot of trouble moving beyond that kiss as well. What the devil had he been thinking? Of course, the truth was he hadn't been thinking at all. Just reacting.

Normally, he thought things through. It seemed that Maggie Ryan had turned ordinary into unusual.

He and Maggie had that explosive sort of chemistry that would be a huge problem if he didn't watch himself. For the life of him, he could not imagine why he responded as he did toward her. She was just too complicated, and he'd promised himself that he would not touch her again.

Headlights from oncoming cars shone through the windshield often enough for him to see her profile. She didn't look a thing like his mother, but she reminded him of his mother every time he caught a glimpse of her face in the bright light. His mother had been unique—not something an English schoolboy considered a good thing.

Maggie's face was unique, too. Different from the British girls he'd grown up around. Staring at Maggie, he decided her looks were even more exotic than his mother's. Where his mother's hair was an Irish bright red and her skin as milky colored as clotted cream, Maggie's hair was deeply auburn, with shiny copper highlights, and her skin tone was the golden color of summer sunlight.

She'd been right. Her looks were as much of a mishmash as her accent, but the total effect was stunning. Particularly her eyes. She looked at him for a moment, and once again, Colin found himself drawn into their mystical, green depths. The intimate exchange left him shaken.

Why had he ever considered traveling home with her? Yes, he was desperate to know more about his brother and the way he had died. But he should have found some other way. It seemed she was one of those vivacious and fiercely independent women, the kind that ran over everyone with her own plans. And that made her trouble. Just like his mother.

"How much farther is it to your home?" he asked, wishing he could have walked, rather than ride in this confining vehicle with her any longer.

She shot him a sideways glance. "Zavala Springs is nearly a two-hour drive from the San Antonio airport," she admitted. "Just relax."

Relax? Not a chance. He folded his arms and gazed into the complete darkness outside his window.

"Colin, you never finished telling me about your brother. Why don't you tell me now?"

Why not, indeed. At least it would take his mind off the woman sitting beside him.

"John…John was rather a sickly lad," he began gruffly. "But when he was a child, before he turned six and became ill, I wanted to take him everywhere with me. He was sweet and charming. Everyone liked him and fussed over him. I wanted to show him off."

Come to think of it, Colin had always thought of his baby brother as a kind of trophy. Some wonderful possession. A pet.

But he had never considered his feelings toward John in this way before, so why the devil had he thought of them like that now?

He cleared his throat. "John couldn't keep up with me after a while. I'm not sure what his health condition was, I was too young to understand. But my mother's mother came from Ireland to live with us so she could *cure* him. She used natural healing techniques and other kinds of…um…remedies."

"Did it work? Did he get better?"

"I suppose so. But it took several years, and by that time my mother had decided she didn't want to live with us anymore. She and my grandmother took John and returned to Ireland."

He rubbed at the ache in his chest.

"I guess I get the idea that sometimes husbands and

wives go their separate ways," Maggie said softly. "But I don't understand how your own mother could leave you behind. Did she explain her reasons to you?"

He shook his head again, then realized she couldn't see his actions in the dark while concentrating on the road ahead. "No. But I know my parents had a big row about it. In fact, they'd begun arguing every day. I never wanted to overhear their arguments, and tried to hide when the shouting began."

His eyes clouded over at the memory, but he set his jaw and continued. "One day I heard them say my name. Later, when I went to my mother for an explanation, she was gone. She'd taken John and my grandmother and disappeared from my life."

"Oh, I'm sorry." Maggie's voice held a note of deep sympathy that Colin would have rather avoided.

He'd never spoken of this with anyone. Why would he do so with a woman who made him uncomfortable?

"What did your father have to say? Did he explain?"

Well, he'd been the one to start this. He had no choice but to finish the tale.

"My father was a broken man without her. He lived another fifteen years, but he was never the same. We never spoke of my mother again. But I could see the hurt in his eyes every time he looked at me."

"Looked at *you?* Why?"

"I have my mother's eyes," he answered as he shifted under his seat belt. "So does…did…John. My father and I would speak of John often during those years. John wrote to me, you see, wrote all about his activities and asked about mine. The two of us carried on a grand correspondence throughout school. He was smart and funny in his letters, but we never spoke of Mother."

Colin exhaled deeply. "After graduation I suddenly became too busy to bother with a brother I barely knew and wouldn't recognize. And then, while in the army, I lost track of him."

"You're too hard on yourself. I think it's normal for young people to want to find themselves for a few years. I know both of my brothers did the same thing."

Colin had the distinct impression Maggie's family would never be able to completely lose track of her.

"But I don't understand why you two didn't try to see each other," she continued. "After you were adults, I mean. Y'all are family."

Not much of a family, he thought. But he wouldn't say so. He had already said more than he should.

"We were never in the same hemisphere at the same time," he told her dismissively.

Maggie apparently understood his need to end the discussion of John for now. But that didn't mean she was done prying.

"Did you confront your mother about leaving? Did you ever see her again?"

"Once." The word exploded from his mouth before he could drag it back. "I saw her once. At Father's funeral. But that was no place for…*she* had no place there, dressed in mourning."

After a long pause, Maggie nodded for him to continue.

He finally found the strength to go on. "John didn't come," he started. "Not to his own father's funeral." The idea still astounded him, but things were becoming clearer, the more he'd found out about John's situation.

"I had to take leave from my unit to attend. Come down from the mountain passes and turn my back on my mates in their battles, in order to say goodbye to my father." He rubbed at his temple, trying to shake the images out of his head. "I only discovered a few weeks ago that, by then, the SIS had recruited John for an international drug sting in Mexico. John was deep undercover, and couldn't attend Father's services."

"I see," Maggie said with a catch in her voice. "And now you'll never be able to talk with your only brother about any of it again. That might be one of the saddest things I've ever heard."

Stunned at her words, he stared over at her profile as she swiped at her eyes with the back of her hand. He reached for her, brushing his fingertips across her hair.

"Maggie…" His own voice cracked, reminding him that he'd promised himself not to touch her again. He needed to come away from this experience whole and strong, and falling under Maggie Ryan's spell could destroy him.

He dragged his hand back to his side, and she never gave any sign that she'd known he'd been stroking her hair. Furious with himself over his lack of control, Colin slumped lower into his seat and closed his eyes.

The next morning in soft gray light and under overcast skies, Maggie tightened her grip around eight-month-old Emma and stared down at the grave belonging to the baby's father. For months she and Emma had been coming here regularly, to place flowers on the two lonely graves. But before today, Maggie had spent her time in the cemetery, wondering about the people buried beneath the headstones. This morning she knew a little more about one of them.

She glanced over at Colin. He'd bowed his head, but his jaw remained tight and set. He suddenly reminded her of her father. She well remembered being at her grandfather's funeral six months ago in this very same cemetery. When her father had stared down into the grave of his own father, whom he also hadn't spoken to in many years, his expression had appeared equally sad and distant. She sighed, blinked and turned her face away.

Colin had been too quiet since they'd arrived at home last night. He'd barely said two words, except for asking to come here to see his brother's grave this morning. On the other hand, she'd been eager to pick up Emma from Lara, her friend and neighbor who'd been babysitting, and couldn't help babbling about the baby. But they'd gotten in to town well after midnight, and she had forced herself to wait until this morning to retrieve the baby.

Snuggling Emma closer, Maggie breathed in the fresh, sweet smell of baby powder and no-tears shampoo and felt the tension leaving her shoulders. So far, Colin had been conspicuously quiet about his niece. It was torture not knowing what he intended to do about Emma.

Maggie wanted to ask him but was still too afraid to know the answer. Rather than just come out with it, she decided to wait until the timing felt right.

Before he made any rash decisions, his spirit needed healing. The guilt he felt about his brother was written all over his face, and in the way his shoulders rounded as he stuck his hands in his pockets. She had the knowledge to help him heal, if he would let her. Despite her trepidation about how incredibly attracted she was to him, she still hoped he would stick around long enough for her to help him.

Emma must have suddenly come to the conclusion that no one was paying enough attention to her. She squealed and lifted a pointed finger toward Colin.

"Ba! Ma!"

Colin turned to look at the baby without smiling. "She looks like my mother."

Maggie glanced down at the child in her arms. "I think she looks like you. Do you want to hold her?"

He shook his head and edged back a step. "I know what her father looked like, but what about the mother?"

"I never met her, of course," Maggie began as she bounced Emma in her arm. "But her driver's license picture showed a pretty woman with dark, golden hair and fair skin. Which is a little strange, because their neighbors in Alexandria say she spoke with a heavy Spanish accent."

"You think my brother met her while he was in Mexico?"

"It's possible. But if so, that would mean she probably came from a wealthy family. The richest and most powerful families there take pride in being descended from fair-skinned Spaniards. My own mother's family comes partially from those Spaniards and partially from the original native Indians—related to the Mayans." She stopped talking for a second, waved her free arm widely across her body and smiled, hoping to get a smile in return. "Thus, the stark but beautiful differences you may notice in my own coloring."

No smile came back at her. Colin kept his features straight and his mouth immovable.

"We'll probably never know for sure." She hurried to fill up the silence, as Emma had already quieted down. "I don't see any way that we're going to be able to trace Emma's mother. I suppose she will always be a woman of mystery."

Colin nodded sharply, as though he agreed. Then he turned to stare at his brother's headstone again.

Maggie heaved a heavy sigh. Once again, she was dying to ask him what was in the back of his mind about the baby's future. But he hadn't let himself get to know Emma at all. Maggie wanted him to do that much before he made any final decisions.

"When we get back to the house, you can contact your mother to tell her about your brother's accident." *And that she has a granddaughter she has never met.*

"No," he said without turning. "I told you. I haven't spoken to my mother in years. I understand she knew full well my brother had an undercover assignment that kept him from coming home at my father's death, but she didn't bother to tell me that when I saw her at the funeral."

Maggie wondered if he'd really given his mother a chance to get a word out at all back then, or if he'd run over her with his pent-up anger. "Maybe she was told not to say anything. Aren't undercover operations sup-posed to be…uh…secret?"

Colin shook his head and shrugged. Ah, the poor man. He really did need a good spiritual cleansing.

"Besides," he spun toward her and his voice ex-ploded in fury, "I don't for a second think my brother's death was an accident."

"What? Why?"

"Think about it, Maggie. John was hiding from a Mexican drug cartel. What if they caught up to him here?"

"You really believe that's what happened?" The idea stunned her.

"Put those excellent detective instincts of yours to good use and you'll believe it, too," he confirmed. "And consider that someone tried to kill me twice in New York. Why would anyone care that much about me? I'm a recently retired British major whose father sold off the family properties some years ago. There's no huge fortune. No other family members who might hold a grudge. Why was I the target?"

It hit her then. She should've realized it before. "Because you were asking questions."

"Spot on." He turned and paced the grass, to the edge of his brother's grave and back. "But I'm not going to stop asking questions. Not until I know for certain who killed him and why."

Maggie felt her face blanch and her stomach lurch. She'd wanted Colin to come here to soothe his conscience and meet his niece. But she'd never meant to bring his trouble right to her doorstep.

"You two keep an eye on Emma, okay? I've got something to take care of in the office. I'll be back in a few minutes." Maggie grinned as she stepped out the kitchen door and disappeared.

Colin glanced down at the wood plank floor and his gaze landed on the baby, sitting on the floor and playing with a set of soft blocks. If he'd been in Maggie's shoes, he never would've left a defenseless child in *his* care. But he hoped at least the other person in this room had some knowledge in that area.

Colin quickly stepped back from the baby, leaned against the long countertop and looked at Maggie's brother, Ethan. Ethan, who unlike his sister had dark-brown hair and steel-gray eyes, was drinking water from a plastic bottle and watching him as well.

"So," Colin began. "Maggie tells me you have contacts in the government. Have you learned any new information this morning?"

Ethan set the empty bottle down in the sink and

nodded. "Some. I placed a couple of calls. The first thing I learned is that the guy who was after you—the one known as *El Cuervo*—was found dead in New York late last night. Single bullet through the head, execution style."

Colin didn't much care to hear that news, but he nodded his head. "He failed in his assignment." *The one where Colin was supposed to be assassinated, too*. He blew out a breath. "No question about it, I'm alive thanks to your sister's actions. She—"

Ethan interrupted him. "Maggie is special." He glanced toward the baby and smiled, then lifted his head again with a scowl. "Oh, we all have *the gifts*, but Maggie…"

"You're talking about witchcraft? You believe your family can work magic?"

"Not believe, Fairfax. I know. If you're going to stick around for a while, you'll know, too."

Colin shut his mouth. The man looked intelligent enough. No sense in arguing supernatural phenomena with someone like him. Not when Colin would be needing this family's help with his investigation.

"Did you hear anything more?" Suddenly, Colin felt something moving near his foot. He glanced down and found the baby grabbing hold of his pants leg and babbling softly to herself. He was afraid to move away, afraid that he might accidentally step on the child or cause her to fall over.

"I have a call in to a friend in the Marshals Service," Ethan told him. "The word on the street is your brother had been taken into the witness security program. I'd like to find out what else they know about him." Ethan glanced down at Colin's boots.

At that moment, Colin felt a hard tug on his left leg

and looked down just as the baby began pulling herself to a standing position by the sheer force of her hold on his jeans. Was she allowed to do this? What if she fell and hurt herself?

He held perfectly still and waited for Ethan to say something.

"Just look at that kid, would ya. What a doll baby." Ethan raised his eyebrows and smacked his head. "That reminds me." He stepped over to the door leading to the backyard.

Opening it, Ethan stuck his head out and whistled. Seconds later, a large yellow dog came skidding into the kitchen. The baby took one look and shrieked. Confused and panting hard, the dog lifted its head for a second and then made straight for the child. This animal stood tall enough to dwarf baby Emma.

Bugger. Afraid to do nothing and just watch as the dog ran right over the child—or worse—Colin reached down and scooped the still-screaming baby into his arms.

Barking sharp and loud, the dog sat by Colin's feet, staring up at the baby. Emma quieted down as she silently stared into Colin's face only a few inches away.

Meanwhile, Ethan, who should have been doing something constructive, was standing by the sink, doubled over in laughter.

Where the bloody hell was Maggie?

Chapter 5

Maggie leaned back in her office chair, glaring at her empty computer screen and its steadily blinking cursor. She'd just sent a message to her grandmother and was waiting impatiently for a reply.

It was siesta time in Vera Cruz, Maggie knew, so Abuela Lupe should be available to answer. Soon.

While she waited, Maggie glanced around her office at the stacks of files and unanswered mail. It might take her weeks to straighten out this mess after Colin left and she finally got back to work. But what else should she expect, when she'd taken time off to follow her lead on Emma's relative and left her brothers in charge?

The two of them were both terrific investigators and bodyguards. In fact, Josh was off in Boston right now on a touchy job, guarding a three-year-old child whose parents were being threatened with assassination by one of the scariest terrorists around. Maggie didn't worry a bit about her brother's ability to protect that boy and keep him safe.

And of course, Ethan had the connections that would keep them in good bodyguard contracts for a long while to come. But neither of her two brothers knew the first thing about the paperwork that a business required.

Sighing, Maggie looked back at the screen just as the bell rang on her computer, signaling an instant message. At last.

Hola, dear child, her grandmother wrote half in English, half in Spanish. How are you and Emma doing? You've found the baby's relative.

Abuela Lupe knew things. And anything she didn't know she usually found in her crystals and dreams.

Typing furiously away, Maggie explained what had taken place in New York. And then she asked, Can you see if Emma's parents were really killed by accident or if they died by someone's black deed?

After a moment the answer came back with force. Murder!

Drawing in a breath, Maggie felt her heart stop. Colin was right. She'd already known it—maybe all along. But now the potentially dire consequences of bringing him here were flashing horrible thoughts through her mind.

Before she could calm down enough to ask another question, Abuela Lupe made a further comment, Dark shadows approach. A powerful *brujo*'s magic stalks. You must be wary.

Is Emma in danger? Maggie wrote.

Not today, Abuela replied. But I will keep watch. Today it is the stranger, the one setting your heart ablaze, who is the object of the dangerous forces. You must do what I have trained you to do, granddaughter. Cleanse your house and the man. Add protection. I will do what I can from here.

Maggie was tempted to deny her feelings for Colin. But it would've been senseless. Her grandmother *knew* things. Even about Maggie's own heart. And even when she hadn't admitted them to herself.

Maggie thanked Abuela Lupe and signed off. Dazed, she turned and stared blankly about the room. A powerful *brujo,* a black witch, was after Colin.

It would take a huge amount of effort on her part to counteract such power. Maggie set her jaw and made a vow. She would do whatever was necessary. Take every precaution.

But would Colin accept her help?

Maggie flew back to the kitchen, dying to tell Colin and Ethan what she'd learned. But after rounding the corner and crossing the threshold, she stopped in her tracks.

She had never seen a sight quite like this before.

Colin was holding Emma in one arm while he reached down to fend off Ethan's dog with the other. Ethan stood by the sink with his arms crossed over his chest and a big smirk on his face.

"Uh. What's going on?" She raised her eyebrows at Colin, who straightened, tightened his hold on the baby and shrugged.

She swiveled to narrow her eyes in her brother's direction. "So? What's Seguro doing in here?"

"Seguro? The dog's name is *Sure?*" Colin sounded confused as hell.

"Safekeeper," she answered over her shoulder. "His

name means 'safekeeper.' The same as the name of our bodyguard business."

She wasn't about to let her brother off the hook so easily. "Ethan…" She lowered her voice so her brother knew she meant to get an answer.

Ethan opened his arms wide, asking for understanding. "It was Blythe's idea. When I told her about Colin's trouble and then said I had a *feeling* there was danger lurking about, she insisted I bring Seguro over to watch after Emma."

Maggie tapped her foot and waited for her brother to continue.

"You know how protective that dog is about babies— especially Emma," Ethan added with a grin. "And just look at him. He's making sure Colin isn't hurting her. That's what you want from a guard dog, isn't it?"

At the mention of Ethan's fiancée, Blythe, Maggie let go of her tension. She absolutely adored both of her brothers' loves and the children they had brought into their lives. Blythe was the practical one. The one who thought of everything before you even knew what was needed. And okay, sending Seguro here today had been a good idea.

Maggie huffed and spun back to the dog. It had planted itself at Colin's feet. "Seguro, go sit in the corner." She pointed and the dog's head went down. But he slowly rose and did as she said.

Looking at Colin, she saw him studying the baby as though to satisfy himself the child was safe. It made her stomach jump with nerves. She wasn't sure she'd wanted him to become so protective. That sort of thing could lead to feelings, and then to love. Which could lead to Colin demanding she turn Emma over to him.

But she had wanted him to get to know his niece, hadn't she?

"I just contacted Abuela Lupe," she managed to say past her tight throat. "Let's all sit down and I'll tell you what I learned." She threw a hard glance at Ethan and he nodded in return.

"Here, hand Emma over a second," she told Colin. "She's probably hungry. I'll give her something to eat while we talk."

Colin reluctantly released the baby into Maggie's arms. But the minute the child was gone, he felt bereft. Lost. *Ridiculous.* Why would he suddenly care this much about a baby? He had never even been around babies. Not since… Not since John.

He sat at the big kitchen table and watched as Maggie secured the baby in a high chair. An involuntary smile flickered across his face when Emma banged her fists against the plastic tray.

Maggie quickly filled a gigantic bowl with water and set it on the floor in the corner, next to the dog, who had sprawled out with its paws under its chin. Next, she took a few bits of cheese from the refrigerator and put them in front of the baby. Finally, she reached into a cabinet and found a box containing biscuits and placed one of those on the little girl's table, too.

He was fascinated by Maggie's smooth and fluid movements. Her every motion was economical and no-nonsense. Earlier, he hadn't paid a lot of attention to the fact that she wore slim, tight-fitting denim pants and a long-sleeved knit top that hugged her form. Now he was noticing them far too much.

Watching her bend and stretch caused his body a great deal of physical tension. His muscles tightened in response to each of her moves. But he didn't want to be drawn to this woman in any sense. He didn't want to understand her. He didn't want to see images of them entwined in each other's arms. And he definitely didn't want to *need* her.

At last Maggie appeared satisfied that the dog and the child were all right. She chose a chair on the other side of Emma from where he was sitting and seated herself.

He was amazed to find he'd been holding his breath.

"Okay," she began. "This is not real good news, I'm afraid. Abuela Lupe…" She hesitated and turned with explanations in her eyes. "That's my grandmother Delgado. Our mother's mother in Vera Cruz."

"The witch?" He couldn't keep the word locked in his mouth. Anyway, that was what he remembered Maggie had said about her.

"The *curandera*." Maggie corrected him with a roll of her eyes. "The practice of *curanderismo,* or white magic, is useful for helping with quite different types of needs. Not the least of which is *removing* witchcraft—those curses and hexes that come from *brujos.*"

"What did Abuela Lupe *see?*" Ethan interjected.

As Maggie turned to her brother, Colin saw the sorrow in her eyes. Underneath that he saw fear.

"She said that Emma's parents were murdered. Colin had it all figured out. That was no car accident they had." Maggie's voice grew low and whispery. "She also said that a powerful *brujo* was coming after Colin."

"Him? There's black magic coming here?" Ethan jumped up and walked over to stroke his dog's head, then he turned back. "The Brit should leave now. What did Abuela say we should do?"

"Calm down, brother," Maggie said dryly. "You'll

scare the baby. And no, Colin will not leave here. We're supposed to protect him. That's what we do, remember? Abuela Lupe is working from her end."

Colin found himself on his feet, frowning. "Protect me? I don't need it. I haven't asked for your help. How would you even go about doing such a thing?"

"Calm down," Ethan told him, echoing his sister's words. "What did Abuela suggest, Mags?"

Maggie serenely picked up a cheese cube from the tray and offered it to Emma. The baby pitched the biscuit she'd been mouthing, took the cheese and promptly tried to stuff it whole into her mouth.

Maggie glanced at her brother, then her gaze landed back on him. Colin felt the heat of her stare and edged backward from the sheer power in her eyes.

"Both of you sit down," she said. "I'll tell you what we're going to do."

Later, while he waited for Maggie, Colin gazed around the unusual sitting room located in the front of her home. It was late in the day, and so far it had been a very strange afternoon and evening. But his instincts told him things were about to become stranger still.

This afternoon Maggie and her brother had done what they'd called a cleansing of the house. They'd used herbs and candles and said prayers as they walked and chanted around the outside of the house. A lot of utter nonsense, if you asked him.

Baby Emma had taken her nap as Colin was making friends with the supposed witch dog. The animal known as Seguro didn't act like anything more than a friendly golden retriever who perhaps had training in guarding humans. Yet, both Maggie and Ethan swore the dog could smell black magic and knew when evil approached.

Colin shrugged and stepped farther into the room where shadows bounced around the walls. He'd agreed to come here for one of her cleansings in order to pacify Maggie. Now he wondered if that was the smartest move to make.

Until this moment, he had not seen a necessity for entering the space between these particular four walls. In fact, there weren't many rooms in this big house that he had visited in the nearly twenty-four hours since he'd been in residence. The kitchen, certainly. That was apparently where most of the living took place. And his own guest quarters on the upstairs floor. Both of those were ordinary rooms. They weren't exactly plain. But nothing like this room.

Maggie and her brother referred to the house as old. But Colin judged the age of the house to be no more than a hundred years, at best. Located on a narrow street in a small, dusty town, it stood out from its neighbors because of the pastel-colored, gingerbread Victorian facade. Not to Colin's taste, but cozy enough.

Apparently, Maggie had lived here as a teen with her Ryan grandparents, who had since died. She'd inherited the place. As he looked around, he could certainly see the eclectic Maggie Ryan in this front room.

The floor was exotic-looking polished hardwood. In every corner, herbs and dried twigs had been tied into bunches with twine and hung from the ceiling. Every wall was covered with a multitude of shelves, each holding candles, flowers, or small bottles of what were presumably healing potions. In the far corner, cast in shadow but partially illuminated by candlelight, was an altar. He'd seen many like it in Mexico. Around and above the altar were more candles, crucifixes and those brightly colorful statues of Mexican saints, the same as the ones he'd noticed in the country markets.

When he took a deep breath, his senses were assaulted by earthy, intoxicating smells. He felt a little light-headed, but it wasn't a bad sensation at all. Still, this seemed like a lot of drama and pretense for no real reason. He wasn't sick, so this whole scene seemed too much like black magic. Nonsense.

"I appreciate you agreeing to have a *limpia,* Colin." Maggie's voice interrupted his thoughts. He turned to see her coming into the room, her arms laden with a cardboard box, presumably full of items necessary for this ritual of hers. "Why don't you have a seat while I prepare things."

He found a comfortable chair and sat, but kept a watchful eye on her. "I gather you do not officiate at these kinds of rituals often."

Her back was to him and she didn't answer, so he supposed he'd been correct. "Can you make yourself ready and talk at the same time? I'd like to know more about your family—your heritage."

"Sure. What do you wanna know?" She didn't turn to look at him, but set the box on a sideboard and reached down into its depths.

He wondered how to phrase the question in a way that didn't seem rude. "Well, when we first met, you mentioned something about a ranch called the Delgado. And I've seen signs around town indicating that a ranch by that name must be nearby. Then when you were talking about your grandmother, you also said her name was Lupe Delgado. That can't all be coincidence."

Maggie hiccupped a laugh, spun, and slanted him a look full of mischief. "You think?" She pulled a wide-mouthed piece of crockery from the box, then set the bowl on the altar. "Okay. It's a long story. But if you're interested, I'll tell it first. The *limpia* can wait a few minutes. Emma's in bed for the night and we have time."

She sat on the sofa across from him, folded her hands in her lap and stared down at them. "Two hundred years ago, a man named Don Estaban Delgado received a land grant in the territory of Texas from the Mexican government. His descendents settled here. A few generations later the Texas government gave the Delgados the right to stay on the land forever and titled most of the original place to the family. Actually, there's several of those old Mexican land grants that still continue in the hands of descendents of Mexico's settlers today.

"Anyway," she went on, "my grandfather Delgado was the last in his family. He met and married a *curandera* from Vera Cruz and they had one daughter, my mother. Mama went to a Texas college, fell in love and married an Irish-American by the name of Brody Ryan."

"Your father? Are both your parents deceased now?"

She shot him a quick glance and tsked. "Hold your horses, would you. I'm telling this my way."

"Go ahead with your story, love. I'm listening."

"Mama's husband, Brody, went to work on the Delgado and soon was running the whole place after grandfather Delgado died. The happy couple had three kids…I was the baby."

Colin had to hold in the smile. She was a rare beauty, with her face backlit this way by candlelight, not to mention brilliantly entertaining while telling her tale. Maybe that was her Irish side coming out again.

"My mama died in a plane crash when I was fifteen." Maggie's voice sounded matter-of-fact and she carried right on despite the terrible words. "Daddy had been the plane's pilot, and he was injured. My grandmother—my mother's mother, Lupe—just couldn't get over it. She blamed my father, when it really was a simple accident. Still, she badgered him, and Dad didn't want to listen to her complaints. He'd already inherited the Delgado because of the old Mexican laws." Maggie shrugged a shoulder and looked away toward the altar.

"Daddy was pretty broken up after Mama's death," Maggie continued without looking back. "He sent all of us kids away. I think it was because we reminded him too much of Mama. He sent me here to town to live with his own parents. Ethan went off to college and Josh to the army."

Maggie stopped talking and swallowed hard. Colin imagined this next bit must be even more difficult for her to tell.

"Before Josh left, he and Daddy drove Abuela Lupe all the way back to Mexico, to Vera Cruz—to her mother's family in the mountains. Just dropped her off and left her there. My wonderful, loving Abuela never returned to the Delgado, and that whole fiasco has been a huge source of trouble in the family ever since."

A sudden silent lull in the conversation made him wonder what else she needed to say. He was about to ask another nosy question when Maggie suddenly jumped up.

"Enough with the sad family stories. Let's get your cleansing out of the way before it gets any later."

He quirked a brow, awaiting her instructions.

She stepped toward the altar but swung back unexpectedly. "To do this right, you should be naked. Take off your shirt."

Chapter 6

Colin gave her an odd look but stripped off his shirt. "Whatever you say." He reached for his belt buckle and flipped it open before she could stop him.

"Hold on." Maggie spun around so as not to see any more. "I didn't mean *entirely* naked. Just from the waist up." Though, really, wouldn't a full view of this gorgeous specimen of a male be worth a little embarrassment?

Hot and prickly, she could feel him moving up close behind her back. His scent, a mix of sizzling spice and healthy male, rocked her senses. His heat rushed through her veins and down her spine, landing smack between her legs.

Great. Now she was hot and sweaty and breathing hard. If being within a few feet of the man without his shirt was so difficult, how could she ever hope to complete a *limpia,* where she would have to actually touch his bare skin?

She bit the inside of her cheek in an effort to make the inappropriate feelings go away, then turned around to face him. He was standing too close, naked from the waist up and gazing down at her with a bemused expression.

"Just the shirt then." He didn't move back, and she felt herself swaying toward him.

"Uh…" Maggie forced her feet to propel her toward the altar and away from the temptation of the man. "That's fine. Stay where you are a moment. I'm going to say a few prayers and chants. After that we'll begin."

She took a couple of deep breaths. "I promise I'll try to let you know what I'm doing, and why, as we go through the cleansing. But some incantations can't be easily interpreted. Are you okay with that?"

"Do with me as you will, Maggie girl. I've given myself over to you for the night."

Holy moly. The images those words conjured up sent tingling jolts down her neck. He just had to stop saying things like that or she might botch this *limpia.* And her grandmother would be forever disappointed in her.

Maggie shook her head to clear it, and went to the sideboard. She dug into her cleansing box for the flowing white robe that was necessary for the ritual, put it on over her jeans and adjusted it so that only a few inches of the long material would trail behind her on the ground.

"You look like Mother Earth, Maggie. It's an image that suits you."

She nodded her thanks but was afraid to open her mouth or to study him too closely in the flickering candlelight. It was far too important for her to concentrate. She lit the special incense that came from the sap of the copal tree. Smoke rose immediately, adding scent and a fine healing power to the already close air in the room.

Whispering the proper incantations, she asked the saints to protect him. She begged for nothing to go amiss in her household, and for the removal of all bad spirits from the man and this place. Stifling heat from the candles nearly suffocated her. She felt a new warmth glowing strong inside her, letting her know the saints would do their part.

Completing her prayers, she reached into the bowl she'd placed on the altar. "An egg cleansing will work to clear your energy field," she told him. "It's fairly simple. I'm going to rub this raw egg over your body. Head to toe. Please stand perfectly still."

This was the hard part. A good cleansing required her to remain in constant motion and not concentrate on any one part of his body. Normally, she would have no trouble with the ritual, but on this occasion she would've rather taken her time. Time enough to explore every inch of the man.

Locking the door on her sensual needs for the moment, she took a deep breath and began the *limpia* in earnest. Amazing. As she worked the room grew brighter, even felt lighter somehow. Out of the corner of her eye, she saw Colin close his eyes and begin his own deep breathing.

When she was done, she cracked the egg into the bowl. The yolk was speckled with black. All the bad spirits had washed out of Colin into the bowl. Now she would need to get rid of those dark contents with another special ceremony, outside and far distant from the house.

Turning to pick up the long bundle of prepared dried leaves, she said, "I'm brushing away all the remnants of whatever curses might remain in your body. Okay?"

Colin opened his eyes. His pupils were wide and dark. Edgy.

He didn't answer her directly. "I've never before… This is an incredible feeling. Pleasurable and…" His words ran out just as she began performing the last chore in the cleansing.

Lightly brushing the leaves across his body, Maggie felt strong quivers under her own skin. Something, some erotic sensation, seemed to be passing between them with every brushstroke.

She caught a moan before it escaped her lips, but Colin wasn't so determined. He groaned, fisted his hands against the sides of his thighs, and his head fell back. The bare skin on his chest and shoulders glistened with sweat in the flickering light.

She took her time and moved in closer, cherishing the tight arousal of pulsating life she felt deep within her body. Guiding the leaves along his skin and then through the tufts of hair on his chest, she began to notice the many scars marring his body. Some were shallow and seemed recent. Others looked deep and old.

She wanted to touch. Wanted to place her fingertips against the points where he had felt pain. To soothe the memories of bad times. Perhaps even to draw out the old aches and replace them with pleasurable stimulation.

He slowly raised his head and opened his eyes. The heat she saw in their dark depths was exciting but dangerous. Her nipples went rigid, pressing against the confines of her shirt and robe.

His gaze lowered, drawn to her chest and the physical proof of what she was feeling. She lowered her own gaze to the zipper of his jeans and found a proof of her own. They were in this together.

But it was all too much. Too hot. Too sensual.

Dropping the bundle of leaves, along with all pretense of completing the cleansing, she stood on tiptoe and placed her lips against his. He groaned again. This time the sound came from his gut. He clutched at her shoulders and deepened the kiss.

She opened for him, even knowing how dangerous a game she was playing. This was all wrong. He was all wrong. She never did these sorts of things, and to be doing them with Colin was plain stupid.

He pulled her tighter to him, and she automatically rubbed up against him, needing to get closer. Wanting the material between them to disappear, she found herself panting and begging in soft mewling sounds. She ran her hands over his shoulders, relishing the opportunity to touch what had been forbidden only minutes before.

His skin felt so good. But her mind kept telling her to stop before it was too late.

"I want you naked," he commanded softly as he dragged the heavy robe up and over her head. "I want…I want…"

Giving up the fight, she started to lift her T-shirt, anxious to be rid of everything standing in her way— when she heard it. Soft at first. And distant. But growing more and more demanding.

"Emma." She stepped back and widened her eyes. "Oh my gosh, the baby's crying. I have to go."

Colin spent a most miserable night, and this morning wasn't turning out much better. He shifted to look at Maggie's profile as she drove them across town to the county sheriff's office. Her jaw was set and her eyes focused on the road.

He turned his head to check on Emma in the baby seat installed safely in the back. He didn't fault the child for interrupting them last night. In fact, he rather thought her cries might have been a blessing in disguise.

His mind wandered back to yesterday's late hours and the ritual he'd survived. Those hazy images drew his chin back around to stare over at the woman driving. His gaze landed on the silky auburn curls, as they lay softly against her shoulders. They made him think of the picture she'd made last night through the smoke, in her robes, and with that earnest fervor on her face. He must have made quite a picture himself, standing there before her altar with sweat dripping from every pore. He'd been mesmerized, watching her every move while she worked over him to cast out the evil shadows. It'd been one of the most erotic nights of his entire life, and he hadn't even seen her naked.

After she'd left him and dashed up the stairs to answer his niece's cries, Colin had blown out all the candles and checked the door and window locks one more time. He'd spoken to the dog and then climbed the stairs. One foot in front of the other. But for hours, his body continued to tingle and his mind raced as he tossed and turned in his single bed.

She was tough but sensual, this witch of his. And she kept coming up with things that jumbled his mind. Not only her *limpia*, which instead of just a cleansing had become a sexy prelude to a missed night of sin. She'd also boggled his mind when they'd first met, with just the idea that she could find him in New York when it seemed beyond the realm of possibilities.

This morning she'd given him a protection charm, an amulet in the shape of a hand with five oversized fingers. Then Colin had taken a step of his own and contacted his embassy. They'd promised to notify someone higher up in the United States government of what he'd learned, and that he had been assaulted.

Maggie had also decided that they should inform the local sheriff of her grandmother's suspicions concerning John's death, and then tell the authorities that the drug lord might be lurking nearby. Colin wasn't so sure that was a good idea. Was the sheriff aware of her grandmother's strange notions?

Maggie swore she'd known the sheriff all her life and he would help them. Colin finally agreed it might be as good a first move as any.

Colin was a leader of men. He'd been born to take command. But he had decided to take a leap of faith and follow her lead for a while. Just until he could compose his mind. Though that didn't mean he liked the idea.

He needed to find John's killer. Needed to learn the whole story of what had happened that took his brother before his time. But he was beginning to need Maggie, too, and that idea shook him to his foundations.

"We're here." Maggie pulled in front of a concrete, single-story building surrounded by a parking area, and parked her SUV.

She flipped open her seat belt latch and turned to him. "Don't look so forlorn. Sheriff Bart Ochoa is a good ol' boy. I've known him all my life. He'll help. Just let me do the talking."

Colin nodded and got out of the SUV while she unbuckled Emma. He came around the truck to help her. But she twisted out the door in one fluid motion and shoved the child at his chest.

"Here. You carry the baby."

"Me? Why me?" He took the load, arranging the child in the crook of his arm as Emma stared up at him with bright, wide eyes.

Maggie patted him on the arm. "It'll be good for you. You'll see."

Good for him. Right. About the same as a dose of his Irish granny's nasty-tasting summer tonic.

As Maggie led the way through the double doors of the sheriff's office, a young Latin man in a khaki uniform stepped out from behind the counter and greeted her. This person certainly could not be someone she would've described as old.

"Ms. Ryan." The man came forward with his hand outstretched. "I'm Deputy Vincente Gutierrez. Nice to meet you. Sheriff Ochoa was called away and asked me to take your report. Let's go on back to the sheriff's office and have a seat." The deputy had spoken with a rather heavy Spanish accent, but his words were clear enough.

"Oh… I uh…"

Colin wasn't standing that close to Maggie, but he could feel her disappointment in his very bones. Perhaps he had become too attuned to the beautiful young woman. Wanting her was one thing. But understanding her was quite another. He didn't want to become intimate enough to know what she was feeling.

"All right," she replied, giving him a half smile. "I suppose we can talk to you. But first let me introduce my friend, Colin Fairfax, from England. He'll be sitting in with us, if that's okay."

The deputy tilted his head to regard him and Emma. But he did not issue any greetings. Instead, the young deputy silently studied them both for a shade too long.

Colin's arms were full of baby Emma, but he inclined his head and said, "Deputy Gutierrez."

"*Sí, señor.* If you'll follow me?" Gutierrez gathered himself up, spun and headed off toward an office in the very back of the large room.

The rest of their little troop marched after the deputy. Emma was surprisingly quiet, with her blue eyes wide and seeming to take in everything. The group moved past cubbyholes containing empty desks, computers and various other electronics, but few people. Colin's initial reservations came back full force.

After they'd seated themselves around the sheriff's desk, the deputy began, "Sheriff Ochoa explained what you wanted to talk about, Ms. Ryan. I was out of town last spring at a special Texas deputy's academy, and I never became involved in the accident investigation. But I heard it was a terrible, terrible thing."

"Yes, it was horrible," Maggie told him. "We have good reason to believe Mr. Fairfax here is the brother of the man who died."

"Oh?" The deputy lowered his eyes and looked at his shoes. "*¡Qué lástima!*" Then he raised his chin again. "So sorry, *señor.* How can I be of help?"

Colin didn't care for the man. Something in his eyes said he wasn't sorry a bit, despite his words. But Colin had promised Maggie he wouldn't say anything unless she asked him a question. So he continued to sit in silence as he rocked Emma.

"My *abuela…*" Maggie began hesitantly. "Um…has anyone said anything to you about my family? About the Delgado-Ixtepan heritage?"

Colin felt she was deliberately speaking to the deputy in English instead of Spanish, and he knew it was probably for his benefit. As he rocked Emma in his arms and listened, he thought he could've kept up.

"*Sí*... No." The deputy rubbed the back of his neck. "I have heard rumors."

"It's all right, Deputy," Maggie said soothingly. "No need to be embarrassed. My grandmother, Lupe Delgado, is a famous *curandera* living in Vera Cruz. And for over thirty-five years she lived on the Delgado and was a healer to the people. Everyone around these parts knows of her."

Maggie stared directly into the deputy's eyes and by the sheer power of her personality forced him to gaze at her in return. "My grandmother's mother, Maria Elena Ixtepan, is also very famous. Perhaps you have heard of the black witch of Vera Cruz?"

Colin watched the deputy go pale. He had obviously heard the name. But Colin hadn't, and he wondered if there was a reason that Maggie mentioned her great-grandmother to this man now, and not to him.

The deputy swallowed hard enough so that his Adam's apple bounced up and down in his throat. He did not answer directly but nodded that he knew of the black witch. Colin imagined that the man was not happy to hear of her again, either.

"Good," Maggie said with a sharp nod. "That's good. Then you will understand when I say she *knows* that the car accident of Mr. Fairfax's brother was not a real accident. The brother and his wife were murdered."

The deputy blanched. But once again, Colin caught something there that said he was not at all surprised to hear the news.

"What do you wish the sheriff to do about this, *señorita?*" The deputy's voice was unwavering, and Colin decided that was telling.

"I want Sheriff Ochoa to reopen the investigation. Maybe someone saw something and just hasn't come forward. Mr. Fairfax wants to know the truth and he wants the guilty to pay. My grandmother and I intend to help him, and we have taken steps to protect him. *Comprende?*"

The man nodded again and shifted his eyes toward Colin and the baby. Suddenly, the deputy stood and raised his fisted hands. But once on his feet, he must have realized he was the only one standing and dropped his hands meekly to his sides.

"I will report this to the sheriff. Is there anything else?"

Maggie stood and joined the deputy. "No. Not right now. But, thanks." She swung around and held her hands out to Emma.

The baby took one look at the woman who was the only mother she'd ever known and literally jumped from Colin's arms into Maggie's outstretched hands with a tiny shriek of delight. Without the warmth of the baby next to his chest, Colin felt the air chill. A sense of isolation came over him.

Refusing to give in to the unusual notions, Colin stood, too. And though he had massive reservations about the whole conversation, he shook the deputy's hand. "Thank you, Deputy Gutierrez."

About an hour later, out under the trees beyond the sheriff's station parking lot, Deputy Vincente Gutierrez spoke quietly into his cell phone. "*Sí. Sí, Jefe.* The man you seek is here. I have spoken to him."

"Then you know where to find him," the drug lord confirmed with glee. "I want him eliminated. As soon as you can arrange it."

"But he is under the protection of a witch, *Jefe*. I do not have the power to do you this favor."

Vincente wished with all his heart that he could ignore this drug lord's orders from here on out. Once, six months ago, Vicente's heart had been filled with revenge. He'd been angry and ready to destroy the U.S. agent they said had caused the death of his mother and sister. But it was a terrible blow when, days later, Vincente had learned he'd also killed the agent's wife. And now, seeing that agent's family grieving for their losses, his heart filled with regret.

The *jefe* interrupted his thoughts with a warning. "Where there is strong desire, a way will be found."

Yes, that was a threat. It always came. Vincente knew he would continue paying for his sins at the hands of this dangerous man, with his soul.

The *jefe* must have heard fear in his silence, for the drug lord continued. "I will work my own magic, *mi amigo*. I am a *brujo* without equal. You watch the man. I will contact you when all is clear and the deed may be done."

Vincente cleared his throat, worrying that the *jefe* could see him and would know his thoughts through the long-distance winds.

"Is there something else?" the drug lord asked warily.

"No, *Jefe*. Nothing." But that was not the whole truth. Vincente could not bring himself to tell this evil man that he had also found the baby the *jefe* had been seeking.

Still, the *jefe* would learn the truth soon enough. Vincente knew it. And he dreaded what would be asked of him then.

Chapter 7

"You're sure you don't mind if I drive?" Colin asked.

Maggie never let anyone drive her SUV. Ever. But when Colin had first asked if he could be the one to drive to her brother Josh's ranch, she found she couldn't say no.

"Yep, that's fine."

She knew perfectly well why it was so hard to let someone else take the wheel. It was the loss of control, and the absence of anything to do with her hands. Putting her elbow on the windowsill, she scooted her bottom around to find a more comfortable spot in the unfamiliar passenger seat.

"I appreciate the opportunity," he said quietly. "It's difficult being in such unfamiliar territory and not having any control over my destiny."

No kidding.

"Driving helps." He looked out his side window for a

second and then returned his gaze to the road ahead. "This is certainly interesting countryside. I've never seen much of Texas before, except from the Dallas airport."

A short, hiccupped laugh erupted from her throat. "Aren't all airports about the same the world over?

Glancing her way for a second, he smiled. "Just about." His words matched her accent almost perfectly.

He was teasing, and that usually drove her nuts. But somehow, coming from Colin, the teasing seemed more good natured, and…hmm…sexy.

She threw a quick glance back at Emma to satisfy herself that the baby was sleeping peacefully. Then Maggie gave a fleeting thought to taking a nap herself. She hadn't slept more than a few minutes last night. But trying to sleep now would be a lost cause.

"How far away is your brother's ranch?"

"Josh owns the original Delgado homestead house. It's located smack in the middle of the property that's known as the Delgado Ranch today." She studied his profile as Colin kept his eyes on the road ahead. "Originally, the house, barns, outbuildings and about sixty acres of land were where Don Estaban Delgado set up housekeeping almost two hundred years ago. The homestead belonged to my Abuela Lupe," Maggie added. "It was passed down through the Delgado family. But Abuela gave it to Josh and his new wife a few months ago."

"You mean to say that thousands of Delgado acres completely surround your brother's place?"

"Oh, yeah. So once we cross onto Delgado ranch land, we'll still have to drive about thirty more miles."

"I see." Colin tapped his fingers on the steering wheel. "It must be lonely living out there. Didn't you say that your brother was away on a bodyguard job? Is his wife there all by herself?"

Maggie was surprised that the concept of isolation had occurred to Colin. It was something all rural people, especially Texans, had to learn to accept. But he came from Britain, where the space between neighbors was generally walking distance.

"Actually," she began, wondering how to explain, "I'd bet Clare—that's my sister-in-law—would love a little alone time right about now. Her son is nearly three, and man, what a house on fire he is. He runs all day long. And then she's also responsible for the many ranch hands that work and stay on the place." Maggie sighed just thinking about everything her sister-in-law put up with. "But Clare handles it all with grace and humor. Josh and Clare are raising a new line of horses for my father and the Delgado Ranch. It takes a lot of work and a lot people to make it happen."

Colin nodded. "So…the horses are why we're on our way out there. Isn't that what you said?"

Maggie pointed out the turn onto the Delgado land right then. Colin steered over the cattle guard and under the twenty-foot-high Delgado sign. Soon the rolling countryside brought familiar vistas. She'd played in these fields as a kid. Ran over some of them in bare feet when the spring wildflowers were in bloom. And rode over them all on her horse, chasing after imaginary bad guys, or riding away with an imaginary prince.

She buried her memories as she turned away from the brown, wintry views outside the window and tried to answer his question. "We're going to my brother's because one of the mares is sick with something the vet hasn't been able to cure. I told Clare I'd try a *curandera* cleansing and potion on the animal. I just hope it works."

"You're not an animal doctor," he said with a note of skepticism in his voice. "But you work magic on animals as well as people?"

Interesting question. "Of course. Unlike Abuela Lupe, I'm much better at treating animals than people. All my life I've gotten along real well with animals and children. Adults not so much."

That put a smile on Colin's face. "I can't believe that's true. What makes you think so?"

Well, she wasn't about to tell him the story of her one and only boyfriend. She didn't want Colin to think she was a total loser.

"I might be a tad overbearing," she said instead. "You may have noticed."

This time he barked out a laugh. "Ah, Maggie, but that's one of the things I find irresistible about you."

What did he just say?

Apparently, Colin had also surprised himself with the unexpected declaration. And he must be wishing he could take it back. Because a long, drawn-out silence filled the air in the front seat.

Colin finally cleared his throat. "You said your father still lives and works on the Delgado Ranch. You don't mention him often. Do you ever see him?"

A discussion of her father wasn't a much better subject than the unpleasant memory of her former fiancé. But she figured she owed Colin a little information. After all, she wanted him to approve of her and the family, so that he wouldn't mind leaving Emma in her care.

"I didn't see a whole lot of my father after I moved in with my grandparents in town. But about six months ago, my grandfather Ryan died. He was a widower, and I was still living with him and helping him with his private investigator business." Man, it sure was tough to open up about that painful time in her life. A whole lot tougher than she'd ever imagined.

She swallowed hard and kept going. "I think that's why he willed me the house and business. But Granddad Ryan's death brought Josh and Ethan home to Texas after fifteen years away. It's great having them here, but it was a sad way to get them to come home. Anyway, soon after the funeral, Dad helped both of my brothers get over rough spots in their lives. Real bad rough spots."

Maggie was still amazed to think of how much help her father had been to her brothers. Those things he'd done hadn't seemed like her father at all.

"These days, our family has arranged a kind of truce between the generations. Both my brothers and their families are living in houses on Delgado land. And all of us kids have visited my grandmother in Mexico at least once. She says she's not mad at any of us any-more—including my father. Actually, she says she never was…but…"

The SUV bounced over another cattle guard and it shook the whole vehicle. Emma awoke with a start and began to cry. Maggie reached around and tried to soothe her with a favorite fuzzy toy.

Their conversation had been interrupted in a good spot, as far as Maggie was concerned. She wasn't so sure about telling Colin the rest of the tale about her family. Talk about an unbelievable story. Colin would probably think Maggie and her whole family were totally insane, if she'd tried to explain about their curse.

* * *

Colin drove into the yard of the strange-looking house and parked in front. The two-story structure was made of differing styles of architecture, and it looked as though additions had been made by several generations over the years. Colin thought it fascinating. A glimpse into pioneer America.

A slender young woman with blond hair was seated on the raised veranda, but she rose and waved as he turned off the motor. She came down the steps, followed by a boy who looked to be around three years old. The child, dressed in corduroy pants and a denim zip-up jacket, was darker complexioned than the woman. But his fine features left no doubt he was her son.

By the time Colin extricated himself from his seat belt and stepped into the crisp winter air, Maggie was already outside the vehicle. The two young women met by the front bumper and embraced, while the toddler clung to their legs.

Emma began giggling and shrieking for attention from her baby carrier in the backseat. Colin reached in and unbuckled her with a couple of the same quick maneuvers he had seen Maggie use earlier. But he was apparently not what Emma had in mind. Once she was clear of the SUV and in his arms, the baby pointed and raised her voice until the two women paid attention.

It didn't take long until the child got what she wanted. Maggie's sister-in-law eased the baby out of Colin's grip, fussing and cooing over her the whole time.

"Look how big she's gotten. Just in the last few days."

Maggie beamed while Emma gurgled happily. "Hasn't she though. Oh, Clare, I want you to meet Colin Fairfax. He's Emma's uncle from England."

The blonde turned her blue eyes in his direction. "I'm sorry finding Emma meant you had to learn the sad news about your brother and sister-in-law, Mr. Fairfax. You have my sympathies." She smiled gently. "But your niece has certainly brought a lot of joy into our lives. I'll bet you're glad you found her."

Was he? He had not been thinking of things along those lines. A baby was, after all, just a baby. For most of this time, since the moment he'd accepted the fact of his brother's death, he had felt only anger toward John's murderer, and fury about John dying before they could have the chance to be reunited. Colin's anger and grief had left no room to consider the child.

He shot a glance at Maggie and found a strange expression on her face. Wasn't that a look of fear in her eyes? He'd seen such looks on the faces of his men in battle. But surely terror could not be what she was feeling now. Not strong, tough Maggie Ryan. Not here in the safety of her brother's ranch house on such a fine, cloudless day.

Shaking his head to clear it, he looked again. Her expression had changed once more—softened, as it usually did while she gazed at Emma.

"Can we see to the mare now, Clare?" Maggie asked.

"Sure. Thanks for coming, by the way. The old girl's not responding to whatever the vet gave her last night. I'm really worried."

Colin slung the baby's duffel over his shoulder and pulled Maggie's supplies from the back of the SUV. Maggie reached out and took the little boy's hand. "Colin, this beautiful boy is Josh and Clare's son, Jimmy."

Colin had his arms full, but looked down and smiled at the toddler. "How do you do."

"Hi," the boy said with the straight face of one who knows about the world. "You're not as tall as my daddy."

"Jimmy!" Clare still had Emma in her arms, but she nudged her son with her hip. "That's rude. Be nice, or you'll have to go back to the house with Maria."

Jimmy pursed his lips and frowned, no doubt wondering how telling the truth could be rude, but he didn't say anything more while they all walked across the yard toward one of the bigger outbuildings. Once they arrived, Colin saw it was a barn. But he'd never seen a barn quite so big, or quite so new.

The entire area, both inside the barn and in the yard surrounding it, teemed with life and industry. Outside, workers were exercising horses in the fenced yards, while others bathed and brushed horses or led them off to outlying pastures. Inside, more workers were mucking out stalls and laying in a nice fresh floor of hay. Everything smelled new and clean.

These animals were receiving the most expert and tender care. Colin approved. He thought John would've been happy and content in such a place. But the idea of his brother never seeing this ranch brought a new wave of grief, so he brushed the thoughts aside.

Clare turned to him. "Can you hold Emma and watch out for Jimmy while I get Maggie settled in with Louisa, Mr. Fairfax?"

"The name's Colin, and I will. Just show me where to put these things."

Maggie dropped Jimmy's hand and took her cleansing box and medicine duffel out of his hands. "Thanks, Colin. I might be a while. Do you want to wait with Clare and the kids in the house?"

"I'd rather look around first." He took the baby from

Clare as she led Maggie toward an nearby doorway. "I'm impressed with your operation, Clare. Would it be all right if I nosed around a little while Maggie works?"

Clare flicked a quick look at Maggie, then smiled at him. "Are you familiar with breeding operations? Do you know horses?"

"I know good horseflesh when I see it," he told her. "And I…uh…played some polo in my youth—spent a great deal of time caring for the animals."

Both women dropped their jaws and gave him a closer perusal. He would be willing to bet they'd thought he had never even seen a horse up close before.

"Then please feel free to look all you want," Clare said, as she recovered first. "Can you find your way back to the house when you're done?"

"I'm sure I can."

Maggie opened the large double doors, but turned back before she entered. "I don't know how long this will take. You're sure just waiting around for me is okay with you?"

"No problem, Mags. Don't worry." He was looking forward to the time alone. He had some thinking to do.

"Do you think Maggie's all right?" Colin asked his hostess several hours later. "It's nearing dusk."

Clare turned her head, but the rest of her body continued cleaning her son's face with a wet washrag. "I'm sure she's just fine. If she doesn't come back to the house in the next hour, we'll take her supper out to her."

Colin had been giving baby Emma a ride on his shoulders while Clare fed Jimmy. Now Emma began to wriggle and whine. He reached up and pulled her over his head.

"I think the baby's getting hungry again," Clare said.

"Would you mind feeding her a jar of baby food and another bottle while I put this grimy hellion in the tub?"

"Me?" The question had taken him aback, but he recovered quickly. "I suppose I could manage."

"I'm no helljum," Jimmy yelled as soon as his mouth was free.

"You most certainly are," his mother corrected. "But you're going to be a perfect angel in the bath tonight, or else. Your father is coming home tomorrow and you don't want me to tell him you've been bad while he was away."

Jimmy pouted. "No. I'm a dood boy."

Clare took Emma from Colin and slid the baby down into a much smaller, softer version of the chair she had at home. "Let me heat up the baby's food a little. Then my big boy and I will leave you and the baby in peace."

Colin noticed a sly smirk on Clare's face, but he focused instead on something she'd said. "Your husband is coming home? I thought he was in the middle of a bodyguard job."

"He was…is. Someone ambushed the poor child's mother this morning. She was shot, probably by the terrorists who'd been threatening the family. The doctors aren't sure she's going to make it." A sad look crossed her face. "Plus, after the shooting, the baby's father took off, and I can't say I blame him. But before he disappeared, he asked Josh not to let anything happen to his son. Josh is bringing the baby here, where he'll be out of the line of fire."

"It seems your husband is quite devoted to the job. Do you mind?" Colin was surprised at the idea of bringing a motherless child here to this isolated place.

"Not at all." Clare inched up a chair so Colin could sit closer to Emma. "You wouldn't even ask that if you knew the Ryans a little better. They're absolutely nuts about kids. Especially Maggie. That's why she started this baby bodyguarding business in the first place."

"It's Maggie's business?"

Clare handed him an open, warm jar of food and a baby-size spoon. "Just fill the spoon about halfway and try to slide it in her mouth while she's got it open."

Emma reached out and tried to grab the spoon, but Colin was too quick for her. He sat back and studied the logistics of this feeding arrangement.

"How do you get her to open her mouth?"

"Well, you can try opening your own and maybe she'll mimic your actions." Clare opened her mouth and Emma reacted by opening hers, too. "There, see? And the answer to your question is yes. The bodyguard business is all Maggie's. The rest of the family pitches in to help, because every one of us feels strongly about protecting the children. But Josh and I are also trying to establish our breeding business, and Ethan and Blythe are working long hours with the Delgado oil interests."

"And each of you also takes care of your own children as well?"

"Of course. But for a good example of never-ending energy we have only to look to Maggie. She makes working round the clock look easy. She's a rock. Does everything without help." Clare sighed, then smiled again. "I have Josh and loads of helpers. Ethan and Blythe have each other and an eight-year-old daughter who talks and acts like she's going on thirty. Maggie just does her job alone and takes care of the rest of us."

Both Jimmy and Emma began to whine at the same time. "I'd better get this young man into his bath," Clare said as she lifted Jimmy into her arms. "You'll be fine with Emma's feeding. Just don't take it too seriously. Everything is washable, and we'll give her another bottle when I'm done with Jimmy. She won't starve." With that, Clare whisked a kicking Jimmy out of the room.

Colin sat stared at the spoon in his hand and then at the baby sitting across from him, who had fixed him with her own sober stare. What had Clare meant about not taking it too seriously? Of course this was serious. The child needed feeding, and he was just the man who could do the job.

Maggie tiptoed into Josh and Clare's front room. It was pitch dark outside and the warmth and cozy atmosphere in the old Delgado homestead made her suddenly remember her aching bones. She'd worked with Louisa for four straight hours. But Maggie was sure the sweet animal had turned the corner and was at last on the other side of her illness.

It was good knowing she'd done all she could to help a living being. But she wondered whether Colin would be upset about her leaving him to fend for himself for so long.

She rounded the corner into the big open room that led to Clare's kitchen. The lights were low and Colin sat in Josh's reading chair, cradling Emma and feeding her a bottle. The sight stopped Maggie cold.

Holy moly. Staring at the man with a baby caused a sudden ache to blossom in her chest. Colin and Emma looked enough alike that they could easily be father and daughter.

Colin gazed down at the baby with a gentle tenderness Maggie had never seen in his eyes. Looking closer, she noticed Emma had on the change of clothes she'd brought—and didn't it also appear as if both man and baby had recently showered?

Maggie sighed when Colin whispered something softly to the baby, who sucked sleepily at her bottle. Just look at that. There was love growing between them. It was as plain to Maggie as the freckles on her own face. But Colin falling in love with Emma wasn't exactly what Maggie had hoped for.

If he fell for Emma, loved her, wanted her, would he be willing to leave her in Zavala Springs? Probably not, and that idea terrified Maggie.

But who could fault him for wanting the baby? Not her. She wanted Emma so much that it drove her to do things she might never have attempted in the past.

Standing in the doorway and watching the two of them, Maggie began to consider a new plan. Would it be too much of a hardship to work on making Colin want *her* as much as he wanted the baby? The two of them were far too different for love to ever develop between them. But if he wanted Maggie and learned to care for her, would that be enough to convince him she was worthy of being the baby's guardian? Could Maggie pull it off?

Maybe. And wouldn't it be interesting finding out?

Chapter 8

It was after midnight when Colin drove off the Delgado property and headed back to Zavala Springs. He glanced over at a dozing Maggie and felt a kick deep in his gut. Even while sound asleep and not making any overt movements, she was a temptation. He imagined doing things to her and with her that would bring them both to life with delicious and heart-pounding sensations.

After bidding Clare good night, he'd barely secured Emma in her baby seat and started the SUV when both the child and Maggie drifted off to sleep. Just glancing over at the spent *curandera* made his chest swell with an odd sense of pride. The beauty sitting beside him was a gem of womankind, even considering her unorthodox beliefs.

Maggie made a fantastic mother to baby Emma. She also ran her own business, one specifically designed not for the money she could make, but to care for children in need. And, remarkably, she'd managed to stop everything else in her life to come to the aid of an animal in distress. Her family adored her and she had neighbors and friends willing to stand by her side.

Colin realized he'd become one of those friends, and he was glad of it. Still, his body clamored to do more than just stand beside her during troubled times. However…

Erotic ideas like that one were putting him on edge again, so he looked through the windshield for something with which to distract himself.

A nice, quiet evening for a drive in the countryside, he thought as he glanced out at the moonlit landscape. He had the urge to reach over and take Maggie's hand in his own. And to quietly let her know that he was here beside her in case of need. But all too soon, the complete and utter darkness beyond the headlights, and the lonely views of a barren stretch of road, served to further his wariness.

Something felt off. He couldn't put his finger on where the trouble lay, but he'd had these same internal early warning signals right before a firefight in Afghanistan. Call it instinct. Call it a gift from his weird Irish witch of a mother. He just *knew*.

Out of nowhere, a tiny ping clunked from somewhere underneath the SUV's carriage. Not loud enough to mean he'd run over anything. And not a thing had appeared in his headlights before it happened, either. It took another moment or two before he noticed the SUV dragging off to the left. Well, he must have run over something. And now the SUV was developing a flat. Whatever he'd hit couldn't have been much of anything or he would've felt a bigger impact. If he was lucky, maybe he could baby the low tire long enough to make it to town.

Before he could take his foot off the gas and ease on the brake, however, a huge black truck appeared out of the dark night. It drove up right beside them without the benefit of its headlights. The enormous vehicle was one of those oversized four-door trucks with jacked-up monster tires. But this one seemed bigger. Badder. Blacker. Its passenger windows had been darkened, which gave it an eerie, ghost-like appearance.

With nothing but moonlight for him to judge how close the truck was to the SUV, Colin still knew the driver's intentions. Instinctively, he felt them inching closer and closer.

In the next instant, the truck's right front bumper nudged into his left front, sending the already hard-to-steer SUV careening off to the right.

He struggled with the wheel, trying to steer them onto the shoulder, and in the meantime pumping frantically on the brake. Rough terrain appeared straight ahead instead of off to his right where it belonged. Bugger. He was running out of room to stop.

From the corner of his eye he saw Maggie sit up in her seat. Her eyes popped open as she tried to take in where she was. Colin didn't imagine she would have time to come to her senses before the SUV would run off the road. But he was wrong.

"There's an arroyo out there," she screamed. "Brake now!" She reached over and jerked the wheel hard right as he automatically stood on the brake in response to her warning.

Colin was positive the SUV would roll with the sharp way they'd braked and turned. But when the vehicle's front tires hit sand on the other side of the asphalt shoulder, the SUV began spinning instead of rolling, doing a neat three-sixty before he could finally bring them to a full stop.

As a cloud of dust bloomed around the SUV and he flipped off the engine, Colin was relieved to find they were still upright and in one piece.

But before he could take a breath, Maggie's hands flew to her seat belt. "Douse the lights." She was out of her side door while he did as she'd asked.

She ripped open the back door then and climbed inside the backseat. "Oh, thank God," she breathed. "Emma's okay. Sweet baby didn't even wake up."

"Grab her and let's get out of here in case those cretins come back to check their work." Colin hauled himself outside and reached for his ankle holster and the gun he'd borrowed from the collection at the Delgado homestead. With the .38 weapon in hand, he tried to get his bearings through the dying dust storm they'd caused.

He heard Maggie rummaging around in the backseat and thought he heard a metallic click. She must be having trouble retrieving the baby, but he was too busy to pay attention. Searching the landscape toward the roadway, he tried to see the pavement far ahead of where they'd left the shoulder. Where was that truck? And where could he hide Maggie and Emma if it came back?

Feeling Maggie come up beside him, he turned just in time to see the glint of metal in her hand. Emma wasn't in her arms, but Maggie, too, had armed herself.

"Where'd you get the weapon?"

"I keep a gun locked in the SUV, just in case." She clutched what looked like a 9 mm in both hands as she swung in the direction of the asphalt road.

"Uh-huh. Well, stand quiet for a second." When she stilled, he closed his eyes and listened carefully. "No engine sounds." Colin wasn't so sure that meant anything. A few seconds ago, he'd almost begun to believe that the truck had been sent from the devil and had just appeared out of the mists—so maybe it could also run without noise.

Maggie lowered the weapon. "I don't feel anyone nearby, either. I bet those dudes figured we ran ourselves right into the arroyo. They probably imagine we're already goners."

"Where's the arroyo?"

Maggie turned and pointed in the same direction the SUV was now pointed. "About twenty or thirty feet that way."

"Twenty or thirty *feet?*" He spun to look in the direction she was pointing, but saw nothing but more darkness. His brain whirled as he translated her figures into meters.

When he was done, he didn't feel all that steady. Looking down at the woman beside him, he could see she wasn't doing much better than he was. Her whole body trembled. He reholstered his own weapon and eased the one from her hand, before placing it safely in his jacket pocket.

Gently turning her to face him, he put a finger under her chin and slowly urged her to look up at him. He'd meant to give her added strength through sensitive words of support. But something dark moved into her eyes just then. He knew both their bodies were still brimming full of adrenaline and excess tension, but he suddenly didn't care. Dragging her to him, he bent his head and did what he'd hungered to do all night.

He took her mouth in a fierce and savage kiss. She sagged in weak-kneed surrender against him, and kissed him back just as savagely. Losing himself in their mutual desire, he let the fire combust around them with a driving force so strong, it seemed as though he had never experienced anything its equal.

She clutched at his shoulders and moaned. That was all it took for his hands to begin an exploration, touching her all over at once. Her face. Her breasts. He rubbed up and down her back, lost in erotic sensations. Then his hands took complete possession of her compelling bottom, as if by their own volition. Once his hands were full of the denim-covered flesh, though, his next move was easy, automatic. He jerked her tighter against his already hard erection, desperate to let her know how much he needed her.

In the meantime, he continued to drink her in. To sip at the cup of her life's energy, with his tongue probing and weaving along with hers. God, how he wanted her. More, he thought, than he had ever wanted a woman in his entire lifetime.

She reached between them, clutched a handful of his shirt and ripped it out of the waistband. Making a noise that sounded like a purr, she put her hands against his bare chest. Her *ice cold* hands.

The realization that the two of them were standing in the freezing desert in the middle of winter struck him like an ice pick to the heart. He broke the kiss and pulled away, but kept his hands around her waist to help her get her balance.

"Colin?" The tremor in her voice was hesitant and unsteady. Not at all the way Maggie's voice normally sounded.

Biting back a curse, he glared down at her. "I can't believe we're having to break this off for a second time. That might be a record for me. But we need to get back into the SUV and move it if we can. Emma will be getting cold in a few more minutes, with the engine off." He exhaled hard. "And I don't like the idea of being isolated out here if that truck comes back."

Maggie looked up at him, questions and desire still running rampant in her eyes. But she must have decided to keep it all to herself, because she only nodded and turned. After one step, though, she spun back.

"Are you still wearing the amulet I gave you?"

He automatically reached for his throat where the rawhide strap had been hanging right up until he'd showered after washing Emma off in the sink. "No," he admitted. "I must have left it at your brother's house."

Emma tsked at him. "No wonder. Let's go home. I can have a new charm ready for you in a few minutes."

Glaring at her, he snapped, "You think this was my fault for losing that so-called magic amulet?"

As she rounded the fender she threw him another steady gaze over her shoulder and said, "No, but don't take the next one off for any reason. Not ever. I was in the car this time. Next time you may not be so lucky."

Maggie woke up crying. But she never cried. At first she'd thought it must be Emma who was sobbing as if her heart had broken, and she jumped out of bed to check on the baby. It only took one second for Maggie to discover the rivers of tears rolling down her own cheeks. She swiped them away furiously.

Shoot. How strange. Must have been some really bad dream that she now couldn't remember to bring her to actual tears. But as long as she was up already, she decided to look in on Emma.

The clock on her nightstand said it was 4:00 a.m. She'd have to get up in a couple of hours, but Maggie figured it would be impossible for her to go back to sleep at the moment. Tiptoeing into the next room, she found Emma safe and sound, asleep on her back. Maggie touched the soft skin on the baby's forehead and stroked her fine hair. Yes, her little girl was all right.

She stood and gazed down at the angel face. What would she do if she had to give up this sweet child? The answering pain in her chest gave her the response she'd known all along. She would be devastated if anything happened to take Emma away. It would destroy Maggie completely, she was sure.

Maggie rearranged the baby's blanket and then retreated out into the hall. Now she was definitely wide awake—and curious about what she'd been dreaming. But she couldn't remember. She decided to go downstairs for a glass of milk. Maybe if she sat quietly for a minute, the dream would come back to her.

Without turning on the lights, Maggie negotiated the stairs and the path through the living room, using the ambient moonlight and soft glow cast by the nightlight on the kitchen stove. Before she got to the kitchen door, she stumbled over Seguro.

The dog didn't bark or yip, he just yawned and looked up at her.

"Good boy." But the minute Maggie reached out to pat the dog's head, a deep sense of gloom enveloped her in a cloud of worry. "Seguro, go upstairs and lay by the crib."

She wasn't sure why she suddenly felt strongly that the baby needed closer protection tonight. But

Maggie had felt a dark presence that seemed to be…*searching* for Emma. That must have been what Abuela Lupe had felt, too.

The dog apparently knew exactly what she wanted. He ambled up the stairs and disappeared into Emma's bedroom.

By the time Maggie reached the refrigerator, her heart was pounding out an awesome beat. Pure fear. Maggie seldom felt fear. She'd always been able to protect herself and the ones she loved from physical harm. Still, she sensed her dream tonight had been some kind of warning, and it had left her shaken. But a warning of what?

She knew about her dread of something happening to Emma. She also knew about her fear of losing the baby to Colin or his family. But what of Colin? She felt fear for him, too. When they'd first met, she'd been afraid, not *for* him but *of* him, because he represented a potential loss. But earlier tonight, she'd been deathly afraid that he would be hurt.

Why? What had changed? Maggie knew the answer to her own question, though she had fought admitting it. For some time she'd been falling in love with him.

Tonight, the sight of the big, strong military man being gentle and tender with the baby must have somehow tipped the scale over to "already in love." It was fine trying to convince herself that she needed him to want her and like her, *only* so he would leave Emma in her care. But she knew that was less than half true.

She hadn't missed the fact that he thought the two of them were way too different to ever be a real couple. Even she knew relationships between such unlikely backgrounds seldom worked for the long haul. And she was also positive he had every intention of leaving her behind when he was done getting his answers. Yet, deep down underneath the lies she'd been telling herself, she knew she would do anything, say anything, to make him want to stay. Anything that didn't involve magic, that is.

Maggie had long ago promised her grandmother she would never use trickery or black magic on anyone. She'd sworn to only practice white magic, in the way Abuela had taught her. In fact, it'd been Maggie's great-grandmother's black magic that had caused her family enormous turmoil and sorrow over the last fifteen years. She refused to consider using even so much as a simple love spell on Colin.

Oh damn, she thought, as she fought back the building tears. Wanting anything this much was bound to mean heartbreak.

The dream came back then. A nightmare. A nightmare of Maggie in five years, and ten, and fifty. All alone. No lovers and no children. A spinster aunt to her brothers' adopted kids.

Her tears began falling again in earnest. Nothing she could do would stop them.

All by herself, surrounded by the eerie shadows made in the wee hours of morning, Maggie lowered her head to the kitchen table and just let the tears flow.

Colin awoke with a start. He was out of bed and stepping into his jeans before he even registered where he was. What was that sound? So distant and eerie. Yet distinctly melancholy.

Was someone in trouble? Or was it his imagination?

Without buttoning his pants or bothering with his boots, Colin edged to the door of his room and slipped out into the hall in his bare feet. In fifteen seconds he took the few steps to the baby's room and eased open the door.

In the glow of the night-light, he saw Seguro raise his head from the floor and let out a low growl. Why was the dog with the baby? Had something happened? With another glance, Colin saw Emma sleeping peacefully in her crib.

He blew out a breath and backed out of the room before he disturbed her or before Seguro made any real fuss. Still, why was the dog there guarding the child?

Last night's vehicular assault had been scary enough. But if someone had followed them… Endangering Maggie and Emma was something he would never accept. If an evil man was after him, wanted to kill him for asking questions, that was just fine. He could take care of himself. And he would even relish such a confrontation. But the thought of anyone hurting Emma or Maggie… Well, it was unthinkable. Colin would move out and go far away, maybe even give up his quest, rather than take the chance.

Back in the hall, he lifted his head and listened again. The noise he'd been hearing was still there. Perhaps it was the wind. He'd heard these Texas prairies were prone to be windblown places.

But the longer he stood and listened, the more the disturbance he'd heard seemed like a woman wailing. The cries sounded a lot like keening. He'd certainly become familiar enough with that sort of unearthly wail in Afghanistan, when the local women had mourned their lost husbands and children after Taliban attacks.

But here in Texas? Perhaps he should be wondering if this house had a ghost. After everything he'd

been through here, any kind of supernatural phe-
nomenon shouldn't surprise him about Maggie, her
family or her house. He was slowly having to face
some hard truths.

Quietly, Colin went down the stairs and looked
around. The noise was coming from the kitchen, but
nothing seemed amiss that he could see.

The closer he came to the kitchen's threshold, the
more the sobbing struck him as wretched. The despon-
dent sounds made his gut clench in response.

Was *Maggie* crying? Peeking inside the room, he
spotted her with her head laying in her hands on the
table. Her shoulders shook with each deep sob.

Colin was struck by conflicting urges. The first was
to go to her. Comfort her. Take her in his arms and
soothe the tears away with hot kisses and tender
caresses. Whatever had brought on this scene would
never stand up to the sizzling attraction that existed
between them. *He* could barely stand up to that temptation. And he would bet a little relief of all that sexual
tension would certainly take her mind off whatever was
causing her such pain. She would be a most willing
partner, too. He knew it with the certainty of someone
who had been fighting the losing battle himself for days.

His second urge was to run. Bloody hell. He didn't
need this. He. Did. Not. Need. This.

He couldn't need it. John was dead and someone was
trying to kill him, too. Besides, he'd vowed long ago
never to become involved with anyone who came from
such a different culture than his own. That kind of star-
crossed involvement had destroyed his father and
ruined his own childhood. He'd be damned if he was
ever going to…

"Colin?" She'd lifted her head and was staring at him with vivid eyes.

Swallowing hard in the face of such desire, he made his decision, and took the only real choice he had.

Chapter 9

He went to her side. "What's wrong? Is there anything I can do?"

Colin laid a gentle hand on her shoulder and felt the instant pull between them. It ignited his senses and drew him closer still.

She lifted her head and immediately tried to put herself to rights. Straightening, she brushed frantically at the wetness glistening on her cheeks and eyelids.

Clearing her throat, she mumbled, "I'm...I was..." She bit her lip. "It was just a bad dream. No need for you..."

He couldn't bear the stubborn way her trembling chin lifted as she obviously tried hard to be strong. He'd meant only to take her mind off whatever it was by way of a little midnight flirting. Instead, he suddenly couldn't control his own desperate need. He took her by the wrists and dragged her to her feet.

Thrusting a hand through her glorious hair, he held her steady as he kissed her. Ruthlessly kissed her, with more frenzy and passion than he'd thought himself capable of.

Her hands came up to his bare chest. But she held them hesitantly on his skin. He pulled his head back to look at her. Her eyes opened as her heated gaze met his, and her nipples hardened under the thin nightshirt. The idea that she wasn't wearing a bra made his own need to touch her nearly unbearable. His hand was under the shirt before the thought had time to register. Rounded, satiny breasts met his fingertips, and just like that, he was hard and ready. Nudging the firm tips of her breasts with his thumbs made her skin pucker and heat under his touch. She hummed out a low moan.

Whatever his intentions had been originally, the sound of her moan went straight to his head like an adrenaline rush. Suddenly, he had to see her, too. He tugged the shirt up and over her head with one quick move, baring her breasts to his view. She gasped and crossed her arms to cover herself.

Uh-uh. That wouldn't do. He caught her wrists and pulled them high over her head, making her lower back arch and the firm, full globes spread out before him. Then, because just looking wasn't nearly enough, he bent his head and took one purplish nipple into his mouth. He lapped the hard little nub, then blew cool air across it. Pulling, sucking and nipping, the more he tasted and played with her, the louder her responses became. Her hands jerked free and then sharp nails dug into his shoulders, but the pain only served to stir him higher.

Blood pounded through his veins and whooshed in his ears. Blinded by a savage lust, Colin felt his usual restraint evaporate. Somehow, one last thread of civilized behavior stopped him from grabbing whatever he wanted. After all, this was Maggie.

An ingrained self-control gave him enough strength to hold back and take it slow. For her. For Maggie. He lifted his head and looked around. Beneath him Maggie quivered and whimpered in his arms. Her fine auburn hair spilled over her back as she looked up into his eyes with a dazed expression.

Bloody hell. He was no blasted saint, and he couldn't wait until they were upstairs in a proper bed. She swayed against him and he moved without thought. With his left arm he brushed whatever had been sitting on the large wooden kitchen table to the floor. Then, hooking his right arm under her knees, he gently lifted her off her feet and laid her on the flat surface. He couldn't be overly concerned for comfort, not with such desperation roaring in his head. Still, he tried holding on to self-control long enough to make sure she was as ready as he was.

Desperate, he slid his fingers underneath the elastic sides of the tiny piece of silk she'd worn as panties. Jerking them down, he roughly stripped them off and tossed them aside. Then he stopped, momentarily blinded as he gazed down at the stunning sight of her lush body spread totally naked before him. The night-light's glow illuminated her golden skin and spilled glittering crystals over the cloud of her hair. Her green eyes were almost black with need, as her mouth made a perfect O of surprise. Her breasts were creamy, her nipples so dark a red that he could visualize them throbbing for him.

She squirmed under his intense perusal, closed her eyes and opened her legs. He looked down at the rust-colored curls covering the juncture of her thighs and he stopped breathing. His fingers longed to tangle there, but he was afraid of shattering the tension winding between them before she was ready. Just the sight of her already made his mouth water.

"What a beautiful picture you make," he said with a roughened voice.

Opening her eyes again, she lifted her arms to him and twisted her hips. He'd wanted her hot. So hot she would be desperate. But all he could do was stand there, watching her as she got her fill of looking back at him. Her wide eyes held such pure hunger that he felt the erotic burn clear down to his gut. She eagerly reached out, slipped a hand into his undone pants and wrapped her hand around his jutting erection. Her fingers seemed to scorch him. Everywhere she touched he felt her burning desire. She was ready.

But he'd miscalculated. He was too hot himself to wait another second. Vaguely, in the back of his mind, he thought there should be something more. Something that he'd left undone. But he wanted her now, with a mindless need that would not easily be assuaged.

He shoved her hand aside and shucked his jeans, then pulled her to him, gripping her thighs and dragging her across the slick tabletop. He pushed her knees open wide, and then licked his forefinger before wet-rubbing the nub of her sensation. She jerked helplessly under his touch and quivered against his grasp. Hovering over her, he leaned in and guided his hard length straight toward the moist entrance to her body.

Maggie breathed in, then held her breath. She'd

never felt like this. She was vulnerable, yet not exactly. She was a siren of desire, yet not really. Nothing in her life before could compare to this, and she felt lost in her own sparkling-hot senses.

She'd expected being with Colin to be as controlled and gentle as her few previous sexual experiences had been. Instead, he came at her full force, knocking her over with fierce passion and uncontrollable desire. As he held her down and nudged himself against the place pulsing between her thighs, she trembled with need and closed her eyelids. Stars flashed before her in a kaleidoscope of color.

Her whole body coiled and tightened, anticipating the length of him inside her. She couldn't wait, but he held himself just above her and lingered halfway to heaven. She couldn't seem to stop herself from whimpering, and she heard herself reaching higher and higher notes the longer he held out.

She threw her legs around his middle and tried to force his erection inside her body. His biceps shook from supreme tension as she grabbed them for support. He made a low noise deep in his chest, sounding more like a roar of frustration than anything sensual.

"Too soon," he said with a breathless gasp.

Not for her. She locked her legs, lifted her hips and impaled herself on him as deep as she could go. Shock consumed her when she realized how thick he was inside her. She held her breath and tensed. How could her body accommodate this much?

Colin stilled, took her face between his palms and kissed her deeply. In moments, her tension disappeared and she melted into him.

She finally felt him move inside her, probing and

inching deeper. Pleasure and desperation drove her to clutch his shoulders, silently demanding that he finish it. But torment seemed to be his goal. He slowly withdrew, almost to the limit, and with a sharp cry, she wrapped herself around him as tightly as possible.

She clung to him as he stayed suspended just over her core. Then, rocking his hips, he slid in deep again, going even farther this time. Murmuring soft reassurances that sounded sexy but didn't make any sense in her state of extreme frustration, Colin gently picked up the pace. Invading her, surrounding her, completing her. His body was commanding hers to comply. He stroked her arms and breasts leisurely, but the lower half of his body kept an entirely different pace.

She was panting by now, and desperation had turned her moans to wails and screams in a voice she barely recognized. He thrust faster, harder, surging himself upward at an impossible angle.

The spasms inside her began as a small tremor, and grew as the pounding rhythm took her away. Her body shuddered and writhed while she held on and went along with him for the ride. Like a roller coaster, every peak sent a thrill so deep she had to close her eyes.

"Look at me," he demanded in a fierce whisper.

Her eyes popped open while he strained against the looming volcano of feeling building inside her. He stared into her eyes, sending her past her last restraint. Sensation exploded through her flesh and bones. Rejoicing in the incredible feelings, she wondered at the intensity of the electricity pouring through her body.

When he growled, her brain stopped working altogether. Far in the distance, from somewhere above her, he shuddered out a heavy groan. At that very moment, a fog of hazy completion overtook her mind and sent her spiraling over the edge into oblivion with Colin.

It must have been only moments later when Colin shook himself out of his daze. Tremors continued to buffet his body, while beneath him Maggie lay quiet. He rolled and pulled her lengthwise across him to give her a cushion.

Moving was tough though, and catching his breath even tougher. What had he done? Clearly, much more than he'd intended.

He'd never been through anything that had affected him quite so strongly before. Or so deeply.

He was sure no face had ever been quite as expressive as Maggie's during arousal. Her surprise, mixed with furious desire at initial penetration, was a first for him. As was the lustful emotion in those deep green eyes, growing dark and mirroring her body's reverberations as he'd fought to bring her back up. And finally, that astonished look on her face when the final shock waves began rolling over them both spoke to his spirit in a way that surprised him, too. Her absolute wonder and pleasure at what they'd done together made his gut clench thinking about it even now.

He doubted that she'd been a virgin, even though she was impossibly tight. But he would wager she'd never experienced any kind of climax before.

Humbled, and feeling guilty for subjecting her to such animal behavior without first judging what she might have really needed, he vowed to reassure her. To tell her he wasn't a predator or a fiend in gentlemen's clothes. Then, when they parted to return to their beds, he would be careful bidding her a good-night.

That pleasant picture quickly dissolved as Colin

became painfully aware that parting at all might be a little tougher than he'd first imagined. She was squirming against him to get more comfortable and he was already growing hard. Close to desperate so fast, he wanted nothing more than to hear another of those bone-melting shrieks of pleasure from her lips.

She lifted her head and stared at him. Her lips trembled and her eyes glistened. He trailed his fingers over the smooth skin on her back and touched her hair.

This was the time, right after sex, that he usually disliked the most. He hated it when women expected him to say something meaningful. Something that meant they could count on him to stay. He never stayed. He never said much at times like these either.

"You okay?" He swallowed a hard knot in his throat.

"Sure." She blushed, gave him an impersonal smile and raised up on her elbows, preparing to climb off his body.

Wait! She was the one leaving first? Not in this lifetime.

He swung her up in his arms and stood all in one swift movement. Things weren't finished between them. He didn't want either of them to retreat to their own neutral corners. Not yet. A possessive furor overtook him as he hefted her against his chest and stormed toward the stairs.

"Hold it," she said as she laid a hand against his thudding heart. "Where are we going? I'm perfectly capable of walking."

Still breathing hard, he ignored her and managed to take the stairs two at a time. He was grateful for not having to pass Emma's door on the way to his bed. The baby's room was farther down the hall, and Colin thanked God for both the dog and the heavy wooden doors of this old house. He quietly closed the one to the guest room behind him and then placed Maggie on the bed. He slid in beside her and wrapped his arms around her waist before she could say another word.

This time he swore it would all be for her. She opened her mouth to say something and his own mouth covered those luscious lips, kissing her with as much gentle persuasion as he could manage, considering his heated need. He couldn't let her talk her way out of his arms until he proved he could be a civilized lover. He covered her shuddering frame with his own and situated himself between her legs. Then his mind apparently took a short holiday from thinking at all.

Overcome by a sudden blinding need to possess, he quietly and simply sheathed himself inside her tight, swollen core in one swift move. Inhaling sharply, Maggie raised her lids to look at him with unfocused eyes.

The shock of being inside her, of feeling like he'd come home, stopped him for a second and left him without words. He hadn't even checked her readiness in advance, just staked a claim on her body with his own.

She reached up, touching his cheek as he exhaled. "I was too rough," he whispered when she feathered her fingers lightly down his jaw. "I couldn't seem to help it. I'm so sorry, Maggie. This time, I promise—"

"Don't make promises you can't keep." Maggie's eyes suddenly twinkled with promises of their own.

Colin shut his mouth and set himself to the task of finding out what made her smile. What made her scream. What set her aflame.

Soon he found that his voyage of discovery was every bit as pleasurable for him as it was for her. Arousing her with a skill he hadn't known he possessed, Colin learned that the backsides of her knees were nearly as sensitive as the insides of her thighs. He also fumbled into the realization that a nip or two to her toes brought on a feminine giggle in response, which caused a shower of flames down his own taut spine.

Slowly mastering the art of giving her his complete attention, he discovered ways to bring her alive under his touch and with his tongue. He flipped them both over so she lay, once again, sprawled on top of him. Then he encouraged her to lift her hips and slide down on his erection. He wanted her to see what it felt like to be in control. A first for him, this giving due consideration to a sexual partner. But then, Maggie was no ordinary partner.

He heard her sigh. Watched as her lips parted and her eyes closed. She was a rainbow of erotic color, and he nearly forgot to breathe. Bending nearly in two, he took a hardened nipple into his mouth and sucked deep. She moaned low. He honestly felt the static charge run from his lips to her core as the passion surged through her body.

Leaning down almost close enough to kiss his chest, she braced her hands on either side of his body and began swiveling her hips. The bliss on her face was incredible. Her hair floated airily around her head like a halo. She ground against him. Once. Twice. Then crying out in surprise, she stiffened as her climax hit with no warning. Shocked and completely unprepared himself, his own peak came within seconds of hers. He'd tried to hold off, but the spasms of her internal muscles milked at him, and the delicious pleasure became more than he could bear.

He jerked his hips and thrust deep, driving his seed into her depths. Hearing himself cry out, the sound was a whoop of primitive male ownership. All thought stopped while the world spun giddily out of orbit.

When Colin at last came to his senses, Maggie was still sprawled on top of him. He wrapped her in his arms and twisted them both to a more comfortable position. Spooned around her back, he rested his chin on the top of her silky hair and closed his eyes. He felt so sated and complete that when an unpleasant but nagging thought snuck into his mind, he banished it for consideration at a later time. Right now, he wished to just float in the perfection he'd found with this unlikely but extraordinary woman.

Maggie opened her eyes sometime later, as the smoky gray light of dawn peeked through the window blinds. Achy, but pleasantly so, her first thought was of the miraculous night she and Colin had spent in each other's arms. He'd frightened her at first with his intensity and ferocious lovemaking. But not for long. Having her body strung tight with pleasure had made every moment a pinnacle she would not soon forget. She'd never been through anything like it. She was a changed woman.

Mercy. She felt like shouting and running through town telling everyone she knew what it meant to be in love. Oh, what a night it had been. Shifting so she could glide her hand over Colin's now-familiar body, she found only the cold indentation of where he'd been.

Shooting straight up in bed, Maggie looked around at the solitude of the guest room. Everything seemed too quiet. She wondered if he'd felt embarrassed by what they'd done and couldn't face her in the stark light of day. That was something she would've done in the days before Colin, but it didn't seem like Colin's style. So, where was he?

She stood and pulled the blanket off the bed to wrap

around her naked body. A quick check told her that his duffel and clothes were still where they'd been in the closet. So he hadn't taken off for good. She found herself comforted by the knowledge and grinned to herself.

Maggie needed a shower in the worst way. However, it was more important to check on the baby before she did anything else. Her thoughts turned back to Colin as she wrapped the blanket around her. Now that she knew what it felt like to have him deep inside her, she was afraid she might be addicted. And there was every possibility he would soon be leaving.

Needing a moment, she headed up the hall toward her room for a robe. She stopped for a quick peek into Emma's bedroom and froze.

The baby wasn't in her crib. Seguro was missing, too. Uh-oh. Maybe Colin had taken her little girl after all.

Panic squeezed the breath out of Maggie's chest. Had last night been all just a smokescreen so Colin could sneak her baby away? No. She refused to accept that the man who had taken her on the wildest ride of her entire life would stoop to using the passion between them against her in that way.

He might not be as convinced that they could have a future together as she was. But he was a man of honor. A man who would never go away without a word.

She flew into her bedroom. After jamming her arms into the sleeves of her old seersucker robe, she raced down the stairs. By the time she hit the kitchen doorway her heart was crashing erratically in her chest and her eyes had filled with tears. But she'd cried enough tears.

As she rounded the corner, her feet slid out from under her and she pulled up short. Righting herself by grabbing hold of a chair, she could barely believe what she was seeing. Colin, dressed in the same jeans he'd worn last night and still naked to the waist, sat calmly at the kitchen table holding the baby. He was feeding Emma her morning bottle as if nothing whatsoever had happened at that very same table last night.

He looked up at the sound of Maggie's frantic entrance and smiled. "Morning. I was hoping you'd be able to sleep in. Seguro is outside and Emma and I are managing quite well."

"So I see." She moved closer to inspect her child. "You changed her diaper." Maggie was surprised at seeing Emma clothed in her morning play attire and with her hair neatly brushed back from her face.

"Yeah. Of course the nappy still takes us a bit of doing," he said while gently touching Emma's nose and watching her suck away on the bottle. "But your sister-in-law's an excellent teacher. Emma and I had a nice run-through practice at her house. I think we're becoming a good team."

Despite what had happened between them last night, despite that she was falling desperately in love with him, she instinctively knew he was going to take her child and her heart with him and go. Maggie figured she'd better sit before she fainted.

Once she was seated across from them, Colin glanced over at her. "I made coffee. But my way of brewing it might not be to your taste."

"I'll have some later," she whispered.

"Maggie," he began again in a serious tone while he kept his eyes on the baby's face. "We need to talk."

This was it. Oh Lordy. She wasn't ready to hear the dreaded words. *Please don't break my heart or take my reason for living away.*

"Last night I…" He cleared his throat. "Last night was incredible. *You* were more than incredible. While I was inside you, my heart just kept stopping. You threw me a curve, Mags."

She steeled herself. What was coming next?

"I lost my head and totally forgot to use a condom. I'm so sorry. I'm healthy and I have no doubts about you. But I'm guessing you're not on the pill. Am I right?"

"Oh, that."

He looked up then and narrowed his eyes at her. "Yes, *that.* Are you using some kind of contraceptive or not?"

She shrugged. "No need. I…"

His eyes clouded. "Oh, love, don't say you can't have children. I know how you feel about babies."

Standing, she moved to the coffeepot. It was time to come clean with him. "You're right. I can't have kids. But neither can my brothers. Their children are both adopted. It's a family thing. We…"

How could she say this? She turned to look at his stricken face and decided blurting it out was the only way to go at this point. Nothing else would do.

"None of my family can have children," she said. "We can't bear kids because we've been cursed!"

Chapter 10

"Cursed? You're not serious." But Colin could see that she was. Deadly serious.

Maggie nodded, poured herself a mug of coffee and sat back down at the table. "It's a long story. Do you want to hear it?"

In truth, he would rather not. He'd been sitting here at this table for the last twenty minutes, still wrapped in a hazy cocoon of contentment from last night's lovemaking, trying to convince himself the two of them could find a way to put differences aside and become a couple. *If* she'd gotten pregnant. And *if* she would be willing to move away and start a new life with him in London.

Instead, he had to deal with a family curse? He sighed heavily and said, "Tell me."

Her eyes darkened and she stared down into her coffee mug. "Well, first, you need to know a little about my father. You haven't met him yet, but I'd bet when you do, he'll be the epitome of every modernday Texas cattle and oil baron you've ever imagined. Bigger than life and twice as powerful."

She hesitated and stirred a spoonful of sugar into her coffee. "Dad met and married my mom when they were both teenagers. He was made ranch foreman to his father-in-law at age twenty-five. Then, when my grand-father Delgado passed away, Dad took over the whole operation at the tender age of thirty."

"He sounds like someone I would like to meet."

Maggie tilted her head to gaze at him with those bright green eyes. "Yes, you two would probably get along."

He gave her a smile in response and waited for her to continue.

"Anyway, while growing up, I thought the only good thing about my father was the wonderful way he treated my mother. Both my mother and *her* mother were *curanderas*. Different from everyone else. And people who did business with the ranch just assumed my father had married her in order to gain control of the Delgado." She hesitated, looked away and sighed. "But that was never true. My father loved my mother passionately. You could see it in his eyes when he looked at her."

Colin had only to look in the mirror to see great passion in a man's eyes. He found himself being turned on just by listening to Maggie's smooth, low voice.

At that moment she glanced down at Emma with such a longing that it blasted him right out of his sensual fog. "Would you like to give Emma the rest of her bottle?" he asked. "She seems to be losing interest, and I think she's snoozing. We'll never get finished this way."

Maggie's whole face brightened. "Thank you."

She slid Emma from his arms and sat down with her. Maggie tapped her fingers lightly on the baby's cheek to get her attention. Once Emma was awake and alert, Maggie placed the bottle's nipple in her mouth and cuddled her close. Emma cooed and smiled and went right back to sucking mightily.

It was quite a sight to see. The picture these two made together gave him chills. He had to fight to keep from staring at them and from letting his mouth flap open. They were the embodiment of a pure, perfect love.

He worked to clear his head. "Go on with your story."

Maggie actually felt herself grinning. Now that she had Emma back in her arms, things couldn't go too far wrong. If she'd had a choice, she would rather not tell Colin the story of the curse. He must already think she and her whole family were nutballs. But then she'd gone and opened her big mouth.

Sighing, she mentally shrugged away her misgivings. Why not just tell him everything? Knowing wasn't going to drive him away any sooner than he was already determined to go.

"When I was about fifteen," she began. "My dad and mom went to the yearly Oil Moguls' Ball held in Dallas. My father flew them up there like he always did. But on the way home the plane crashed. My father was badly injured—and my mother was killed on impact."

Colin's eyes quickly filled with sympathy. "So you've already said, love. I'm sorry for your loss, and I know it must still hurt. Do you blame your father for your mother's death?"

She shook her head. "No…no. I always knew it was an accident. A terrible, horrible accident.

"But for a time my Abuela Lupe seemed to blame

Dad. At least, we all thought she did. She raged and cried and refused to speak to him."

The memory still stung. Her mother was dead and her beloved grandmother had been too filled with her own grief to console her grandchildren.

"Finally, Dad couldn't take it anymore," Maggie went on. "He and Josh packed up Abuela and drove her all the way to her family's mountain home in Vera Cruz. Ethan and I begged him not to, but Dad couldn't take any more of Abuela's accusing looks."

"That must have been a hard time for all of you."

Talking about it was bringing the pain back. Maggie fingered a tiny tear out of the corner of her eye.

"Yeah," she said softly. "But it's okay now. Let me get back to the story of the curse. When Dad dropped Abuela off at her mother's home, he found out that my great-grandmother, Maria Elena, had become a *bruja*, a black witch. None of us had ever met her and even Abuela Lupe hadn't seen her own mother in over twenty years.

"Maria Elena suddenly became furious at Dad. She accused him of murdering her granddaughter and banishing her only daughter from her Texas home. Then she took one look at Josh's guilty expression and got really serious."

Maggie blinked, feeling not quite strong enough to finish the telling. But then she steeled herself.

"The ancient *bruja* dragged out her potions and devil statues and began putting together a curse so evil it made the mountains quake. She swore that my father would pay for his misdeeds. That all his children would be barren and his name would die forever with this generation. Before Abuela could stop her, she pointed her finger at him again and swore that his own actions would scatter his family and make us hate him."

"And did it?" Colin asked with a wry grin.

Maggie could see he was having trouble accepting her story as true. "More or less. By the time they arrived back home, Josh was horrified that he'd helped Dad drive Abuela away. His own guilt made my brother turn to the army, and he didn't come back. It took my Grandfather Ryan's funeral, fifteen years later, to finally bring him home."

She clenched her hands against memories of the loneliness. "Ethan was so full of anger over our mother's death that he went off to college early. He'd also refused to come home again for those same fifteen years."

"And you, Maggie girl? You were only fifteen. How did this supposed curse effect you?"

Supposed? Well, she guessed the idea of a curse just might be too much for a man like Colin to ever really accept.

"I never hated my father. I still don't. I feel sorry for him. And it wasn't my choice to leave the ranch, but Granddad and Nana Ryan needed me in town. I think Dad was grateful to be rid of me by the time he sent me here. Every time he sees me even now, I know it makes him think of my mother. I look a lot like her."

Colin smiled sadly and reached over to put his hand on her shoulder. "No, I meant—what do you think about a curse that prevents you from conceiving a child?"

Maggie felt sick to her stomach. "I hate it." The words had come spewing out of her mouth with a vengeance. "I mean… I've gotten used to the idea by now. But I don't have to like it."

Emma finished her bottle then and tried to sit up in

Maggie's arms. Maggie smiled contentedly to herself and gazed over at Colin.

"Having Emma in my life did a lot to take away the anger and pain of not being able to have my own." Maggie held out her fingers and Emma latched on. Soon the baby was giggling and sitting up on Maggie's lap. "Just look at this sweet thing. How could anyone stay mad with her around?"

Colin opened his mouth to say something else but just then the phone rang. Maggie was glad to be spared from having to talk anymore about the curse and about her emotions. After all, it had taken everything she had not to blurt out that she loved Colin as much as she loved Emma.

Saved by the bell, she stood and answered the phone instead.

Still unsure about the intelligence of answering a summons from the sheriff's office, Colin came around the front of the SUV in time to help Maggie down. If he was unhappy to be back at the sheriff's station himself, he was totally against the idea of bringing Maggie down here along with him. But, as usual, she had gotten her way. She looked toward the station office across the parking lot and grimaced.

"I'm not thrilled about being back here," she said.

"I know, Mags. I told you I could've come by myself. I am a big boy, you know." He slid his arm around her waist and drew her close, and she carried with her the scent of the earth.

Cedar and incense and candle smoke. She'd been distracting as hell on the way over here, but riding with her was not nearly as distracting as having her firm breasts pressed against him in bed last night.

Curses and *curanderas* aside, he'd be damned if he wouldn't be right back beside her in bed again tonight, too. And every night until it was time for him to leave Texas. No power on earth would be able to keep him away.

She looked over and then actually winked. "Some of your parts are particularly big," she said over a chuckle. "But you know I wasn't going to let you do this alone. Even though I really hated hearing from Deputy Gutierrez this morning. There's just something about that man…"

"Yes, I feel the same. But Gutierrez was right to call. I need to meet with the U.S. marshal who's just arrived in town. I suspect he's here because I called my embassy and told them about John's death." Colin started across the parking lot with her in tow. "However, I also heartily agree with you that it was a better idea not to invite this marshal to come to your house for our meeting. It'll be safer for us to talk at the sheriff's office. You're sure Emma will be okay with your neighbor?"

Maggie nodded as she kept pace, taking two steps to his one. "Lara is wonderful with the baby. She runs a day care out of her house and Emma just loves being around the other kids. She'll be safe there."

Sentiments about Emma loving the company of other children sounded hollow and sad coming from Maggie's mouth, now that Colin knew the truth of what she believed. Sometime in the last few hours he had started accepting the story of her family's curse. Maggie was so unique. So good and honest and…well, special, that if she said the curse story was true, it was true. He no longer had doubts.

At the doorway to the station, Maggie hesitated and

turned to him. "You *are* still wearing the replacement amulet I fashioned for you, right?"

He patted the small silver hand, hanging in its spot around his neck, and nodded without saying a word. He would not forget to wear it again.

Once they'd been introduced to U.S. Marshal Samuel Dodd, Maggie's reservations disappeared. But she still felt uneasy around Deputy Gutierrez. So, when Marshal Dodd suggested they go somewhere for coffee, she readily agreed.

As they walked down the block toward the Spring Café, she began tossing around a couple of thoughts in her head. One of them centered on Deputy Gutierrez. He must have passed Sheriff Ochoa's scrutiny in order to get his job. But maybe she should try looking up more info on him herself. There was just something…

The other thoughts swirling in her mind concerned Sam Dodd. Everything about the man shouted that he was exactly who and what he said he was. Here was a guy who, in her mind, looked every bit the part of a bodyguard. First off, he had the body of an Adonis. His rippling muscles were quite evident under the long-sleeved white shirt and jacket. He had a beautiful, chiseled face, amber eyes, olive skin and clothes that fit like they were designed just for him. And if she hadn't already met the only man she would ever love, Sam Dodd would warrant a second and even a third look.

As they slid into a booth, Maggie decided she must have the most vivid imagination ever. Looking at the marshal's eyes, she would swear they carried a hurt look. Hurt but still gentle. This man would be perfect as a guard for children. Something about him told her so.

But she had to force those thoughts out of her head. He wasn't here to apply for a job. He was here to tell Colin what he knew of his brother.

"I've heard rumors about your unusual bodyguarding business, Ms. Ryan." Sam blew air across his steaming mug.

Their coffees had been delivered and the café was in a midmorning slump. They were alone in the place, save for the help.

"Only good things, I hope," Maggie said.

"Yes, ma'am. In the past, some of us at the U.S. Marshal's Service have talked about the need for such a business. You're developing quite a rep around Washington."

Colin put his hand over hers in a protective move. "What do you know about my brother, Marshal?"

"Call me Sam."

"Okay, Sam. I'm Colin, and she's Maggie. Tell us about my brother."

"This is one of the sorriest days of my life," Sam said while keeping his eyes lowered. "I don't like losing, not when it means a life. But when someone is determined to leave the security program, my hands are tied. As officers in witness security, we only offer help. We're not allowed to insist."

"So, my brother was in your government's special witness program?"

Sam nodded. "*Was* is the operative word. About nine or ten months ago, at our regular contact, John told me he needed to travel overseas. I said that wasn't possible within the confines of the program. But a week later, he was gone anyway."

Colin swallowed down the wave of guilt. There it

was. John had wanted to come home for his help and died trying. Colin's mind went blank for a second before Maggie squeezed his hand and he fought his way back.

"Why was John under your protection? I need to know who wanted him dead."

"That's classified."

"Please, Sam," Maggie said softly. "Colin already knows his brother participated in an international drug sting of some sort. We'll take any other information you can possibly share."

The marshal gave a quick glance around the room, then leaned close. "You must understand, lives are still at stake. The Mexican government has finally begun taking the lead in the investigation. They have men in place inside the cartel. Men with families."

Sam lowered his voice even more—to a barely audible whisper. "Your brother uncovered a connection between the drug cartel we've been investigating and a prominent Mexican politician. A lot of money and power is backing this particular cartel. That makes the group twice as lethal as others."

When Colin felt a slight tic flicking in a muscle right under his eye, he set his jaw and said, "So the investigation continues without John. Does that mean you have someone close to the drug boss? Someone who may know who killed my brother?"

The marshal's eyes turned sympathetic. "There is little doubt our drug lord is the one who ordered the hit on your brother. But we don't know yet who actually made the hit, and we have no idea who gave him up in the first place. It had to be someone in the Service. But that's my job now. That'll be one snake I will force out from under his rock."

"What about John's wife?" Maggie had been sitting

quietly, but now she became animated. "Who was she really? Where'd she come from?"

Sam shrugged. "The woman was a Mexican national John met during the sting. He insisted she go into hiding with him, but he would never tell me who she was. Said it was a matter of life and death that she leave Mexico anonymously when he did, so I arranged for her papers as his dependent. I met her once. Pretty lady, but she didn't say much."

Maggie reached out for Sam's hand with both of hers in a pleading gesture. "Do you know about their child?"

"I didn't until I read Sheriff Ochoa's accident report. What happened to the baby?"

Pale and shaking, Maggie let go of Sam's hand and shook her head.

Colin felt her terror as if it were his own. Maybe he hadn't wanted to become this involved with her, but that didn't matter anymore. It was a done deal. He'd become more than just involved, and he wasn't about to let anything happen to hurt her—or Emma.

"The child is my niece, and I'm convinced she's being well cared for," he said. "Let's leave things at that."

Sam glanced at Maggie, but then shuttered his expression and turned away. Apparently, the marshal agreed to forget knowing about the child.

"I'd wondered why your brother had all of a sudden become so insistent about leaving the country," Sam mused. "Now I'm guessing it was the baby's birth that made him want to go home. I understand becoming a father can change a man's outlook."

Colin didn't know about that. But he did know he would do anything to protect Emma. Not only did he owe that to his brother, he owed it to Maggie and to the baby.

A new question formed in his mind. "Why do you suppose John was headed back to Mexico, if he wanted to go home? Wouldn't it have been too dangerous for all of them to show up there?"

Sam looked a little shocked. "Mexico? I thought John was coming here." He turned and gestured to Maggie. "When I heard he'd been killed near here, I just assumed he'd been heading to the Ryans for protection. I guess I figured your family would've helped them leave the country."

Maggie's whole body tensed. "We weren't in the bodyguard business back then. And I'd never heard of John before the accident."

Sam looked confused and turned to Colin. "But then how…how'd you get here? How in the world would you know about John's murder or where to look for him?"

Chuckling at the man's confusion—confusion he well understood—Colin said, "Don't ask. It's a convoluted story and not an easy one to tell. Suffice to say, I'm here and I'm not backing down until I make sure whoever was involved is punished."

"Maybe John had friends in Mexico he could count on to help him reach England," Maggie added. She didn't seem ready to discuss her witchcraft with Sam, either.

"You might be right," Sam said with a sad smile. "Or maybe his wife knew of someone who could help them. But John wasn't heading to England. He said he wanted to go *home*—to Ireland."

The jolt hit Colin smack in the gut. So his brother hadn't been seeking his protection after all. The idea made his mind reel. After all that had transpired, how could it be possible that the one person John thought could help him the most was their weird mother?

Chapter 11

Frustrated and haggard, the drug cartel boss flicked his cigarette out the window of his limousine and tried to calm down. The *jefe* believed there might still be a way of avoiding catastrophe.

His silent partner, Governor Garcia, had at last learned that his only daughter had run away to America with the traitor Juan. All along, the *jefe* had known it was only a matter of time until someone who valued money more than his life leaked the truth. Now it would be mere hours rather than days until the governor uncovered the rest.

Once the governor completely understood the facts—that his only daughter had been killed alongside her traitorous husband—the *jefe's* life would be worthless. Running would not save him then, though he had moved millions to Spain in anticipation of the need to escape.

The *jefe* hoped he had one small chance left. The child. The governor's grandchild. If he could get his hands on that baby, he could trade the girl for his life.

The *jefe's* witch-crystal visions had told him that the child remained somewhere near the site of her parent's death in Texas. He had just issued orders for the baby to be kidnapped. Not injured, but taken into his custody.

Like *El Cuervo* in New York, his men in Texas had also failed to complete his order to kill the Anglo Fairfax. And that failure was what had brought the truth out into the open for Governor Garcia. Those men had better not fail to get the child. Otherwise, all hope would be lost.

While the *jefe* waited to hear that the child was within his grasp, he traveled to the governor's mansion for a face-to-face meeting. The old saying, "Keep your friends close but your enemies closer," rang with absolute truth. The *jefe* was prepared to take whatever action was necessary.

A lavender-hued twilight dusted the town of Zavala Springs as Maggie and Colin arrived back at her house. She looked off to the southwest, saw shadowy ghost clouds edging toward them and knew the warm air over-running cold would soon bring rain. Overrunning was merely the echoing drizzle of a decent rainstorm. And at this time of the year, the drizzle usually brought nothing beneficial. Just cold and irritating mists floating down out of the Mexican mountains to devil the population.

She sat silently for several moments and thought back over their long and difficult day. Hunched over the steering wheel beside her, Colin was being equally pensive. She knew his spirit had suffered a major blow when he'd learned that his brother had not been headed toward him but to Ireland and their mother.

After that revelation, Maggie had taken Colin out to meet with Josh and to spend the afternoon talking about horses and anything else not associated with murder and witchcraft. She'd made the effort in order to give him something else to think about. But it had been clear from the pain in his eyes that the deep hurt had never once released its hold on him throughout the day.

"Colin," she began as she turned to face him before unfastening her seat belt. "Isn't it time for you to contact your mother and at least let her know about John—and about Emma?"

Maggie had given considerable thought to how she would've felt if something had happened to her child and no one bothered to let her know. Her heart was aching for the mother whose youngest child had been coming her way but never made it home.

"You must," she said. "It's what your brother would've wanted."

Colin kept his face forward, but his throat muscles tightened. She still felt the strong magnetic pull between them, knowing how angry and hurt he might be at her interference.

This was a man used to leading, not accustomed to following anyone else's guidance. A man who needed action. But he was also gentle, with big-guy tenderness toward both Emma and herself. How could she not love everything about him and want only what was best for him? Doing the right thing by talking to his mother was what would be best for Colin in the long run, she was sure of it.

"I'll consider it," he said with an air of finality. Then he took a breath, flipped off his seat belt and turned to her. "I'm giving you fair warning, Mags."

His eyes were bright and full of wicked intentions as he captured her gaze with his own. "While I'm staying here, I *will* be sleeping in your bed. Get used to the idea."

"Oh." The word escaped her lips with a start. His demand was a surprise. But it was clear from his look how much he wanted her, and the thought that he wanted her as much as she wanted him was a little scary.

"All right." It was all she managed to say before finally flipping open her own seat belt and opening her door. "I have to pick up the baby from Lara's house. Can you come with me to help carry all her stuff?"

Colin narrowed his eyes for a quick second, just before setting his foot outside on the caliche driveway. "What stuff would that be?" He headed around the SUV toward the neighbor's home without waiting for an answer.

"Her diaper bag and her blanket, and a ton of toys and clothes that have just sort of made their way over to Lara's in the last few days. I can manage either all that or the baby, but not both."

She caught up to him as he was making his way past shaggy hedges and around both her and Lara's garden plots. Nearly stumbling in the dusk over a low-lying fence meant to stop small critters, she reached out to take his hand. He hesitated, but then pulled her close.

"Stick with me, love," he said huskily. "And let's go retrieve our little girl."

Colin stood quietly in a corner and watched while Emma played on the floor with another little girl about the same age. Even dressed in jeans and a heavy denim jacket, Maggie's compact body teased his senses as she moved around the room gathering up the baby's things.

Throughout their long day, thoughts of last night and his time spent with her had kept him from fully being engaged in the moment. Her brother, Josh, was a good guy who had also served in the 'Stan, the term American fighting men always used when they talked about Afghanistan. And Josh's vast knowledge of horseflesh was certainly superior to most.

Colin should've been fascinated by their twin interests. But for the whole blasted afternoon, he hadn't been able to stop his brain from flashing to other sorts of flesh. Maggie's soft, enticing and satiny flesh, to be exact. He kept daydreaming about how she responded to his touch.

He must be going insane. So many other things needed his consideration right now. A way to ferret out a murderer, for one thing. And giving in to the necessity of telling his mother about John's death. Those were two of the most urgent. Yet here he was, still lost in a haze of lust and wanting.

He'd hoped that having one night of sex with Maggie would've put a stopper to his raging desire. In the past, that usually worked to get his mind back in the game. Instead, he wanted her—had to have her, really—more than ever. It was crazy.

Forcing his gaze and his mind onto less intense things, Colin looked over again at Emma playing on the floor and felt his tension dissipate. John's child. His only niece. His mother's only grandchild.

Colin found himself drifting back in time. All the way back to watching his baby brother playing with blocks in the same way Emma was playing. He remembered a moment…

He had been standing in the corner then, too, watching John, while his mother wrapped her arms around him and whispered in his ear, "Don't you worry, darlin' Colin. Your daddy and I still love you as much as ever. But we're trusting you to be a good big brother and watch out for the baby."

Colin blinked away the moisture that had gathered in his eyes and tried to bring himself back to the present. It had all been a lie in the end. But still, didn't even a liar deserve to know that her child was dead?

"Colin, can you carry Emma? I'll cart all her stuff." Maggie's words dragged him out of his self-induced reverie.

"Certainly," he answered. "Go ahead. We'll be right behind you."

With her arms laden, Maggie nodded, thanked Lara and walked out the door heading for home.

He picked up the infant and cuddled her close to his chest, breathing in her scent. Her warmth and baby-soft smell went a long way toward soothing his spirit. Yes, he thought with a sigh, he supposed his mother had a right to know about this sweet bundle, too.

Lara saw them to the door, but then put her hand on his arm to stop him before he left. "This child means everything to Maggie," she told him in a whisper. "My friend would be shattered if she was separated from her baby. Don't let that happen."

Colin knew that Lara's words were meant as some kind of warning. But he had no intention of—

A piercing scream from outside drew their attention. Emma whined, while Lara gasped and clutched at her throat. Colin felt his heart lurch.

"Here, take Emma," he ordered, as soon as he caught his breath. He thrust the baby into Lara's arms and dashed out the door.

Once past the glow of Lara's porch light, the night's darkness seemed cold and complete. He ran on instinct in the direction of the scream.

"Maggie," he called frantically. "Answer me. Where are you?"

He heard a small groan from nearby and dropped to his knees. Fumbling around in the dark under the thick hedge bushes, Colin at last put his hand out and felt material.

"What happened?" he asked as he pulled Maggie's limp body free of the brush and into his arms.

She lifted a hand to her head then looked up at him. "Someone attacked me. They took the bundle I was carrying and shoved me into the hedge. I didn't have time to... I couldn't stop them from..."

"Easy now," he said, but he wasn't feeling too easy himself. "Are you all right? Are you injured?"

She sat up and inched forward to a crouching position before he could keep her still. "I'm fine. Just scared. But why would anyone want to steal..."

He stood and helped her to her feet. It was all he could do not to run his hands over her body to assure himself that she was truly okay.

"Oh my God, Colin. They must have thought the bundle was Emma. Someone tried to kidnap the baby!"

Hours later Maggie continued to tremble. Her mind kept reeling with crazy thoughts of whoever had attempted to kidnap Emma. She'd tried to be strong. Tried hard to get over her shock and think clearly about what her next move should be. But as hard as she'd tried, nothing seemed to work to settle her nerves.

Should she contact her grandmother for help? Maybe Abuela could look into her crystals and see Maggie's attacker. No, she thought, the crystals were more for present and future events. The past was always cloudy.

Thank heaven for Colin. He'd been a lifesaver. Literally. He had gathered both her and Emma up and spirited them across the lawn and inside the bewitched protection of her house. Once they were safely inside, he had coaxed her into a warm bath and fed Emma while she soaked. It was such a luxury to have someone take care of her and the baby for a change.

No matter what their futures held, she would never forget his tender ministrations…or him.

She waited in her bed for him to finish putting Emma down for the night. She wanted to talk to him. To pour out her fear and uncertainty, and perhaps tell him that she loved him. His rough baritone and gentle caresses would settle her nerves for sure.

At last, he stepped into the room and quietly closed the door behind him. "I think she's asleep. Seguro's with her. I'm glad you waited for me."

"And what exactly would I be doing in this bed by myself without you?"

He laughed and the room filled with the magic between them. Just like that, she was steaming and ready for him. With one laugh. One look. No one would ever be able to do that to her again. Not in the same way.

"That sounded reminiscent of the Irish, Mags," he said as he stripped off his shirt. "You're really something, you know? One minute you're talking like a sensuous *señorita*. The next like a Texas cowgirl. And just then, you reminded me of home."

His eyes turned stark, as he must have realized what

he'd said. The sound of his own words died in his throat. He turned his back to sit at the edge of the bed and remove his boots.

He was so close and yet so far away. She wanted to reach over and stroke him. Just to touch his skin and gentle them both. He was so hard on himself all the time. And he'd been so good to her tonight that she wanted to return the favor somehow.

Through the low bedside light, she could see the scars that last night she had touched and tasted. Desire surged through her, leaving her breathless and yearning. She couldn't stop herself from laying a palm flat against his warm back.

His head jerked up at her touch, and before she knew what had happened, he'd turned and grabbed her by the wrist. It was how things had started between them last night, with him encircling her wrists and holding them above her head. She was completely aroused by him now, and whimpered under her breath. Her body seemed to respond to his naturally without so much as a kiss or even a word.

She knew now what it felt like to take him inside her body, and she began to crave that. A familiar, convulsing pleasure was already spiraling out of control in her pelvis.

"I didn't think you'd want that tonight," he said in a harsh voice, as he dropped her wrist. "You've had quite a shock. It's only been a few hours since you were attacked. Let me just hold you and soothe you to sleep."

"You would do that for me? But I thought you said…"

He slipped off his jeans and slid under the covers. "I said I would be sleeping in your bed. Let's leave it at that tonight. Come here."

She snuggled close, but the thudding beat of his heart told her he was nowhere near ready for sleep. Neither was she. His heady male scent filled her nostrils with a hint of erotic gratification, and it left her wanting more. She rubbed her hand down his chest, and his muscles bunched under her fingertips. Her thumb flicked over his nipples and she felt a jolt rock right through him. It rocked through her, too, and she heard herself sigh in response.

He pulled back slightly to look into her face. "That's not exactly what I would call soothing. What do you want?"

Now, that was easy. She pulled his head down and kissed him. Let him kiss her. Their kisses were like a Thanksgiving feast, feeding her need.

In the next moment, her hand slid down his body and touched the body part that was jutting toward her belly. It was a shock when she closed her hand around the tip and realized how big he already was, and how slick and ready. Her fingers trailed down the long, smooth column and cupped the heavy mounds at the base. They tightened at her touch and he drew in a breath.

She heard herself humming low in her chest as she closed her hand around his pulsating erection. The need to taste instead of touch was too tempting.

She scooted down his body until she was close enough to take the tip into her mouth. But he responded by exploding with a string of curses and rolling them over faster than she could blink.

When he had her underneath him and hovered over her body, she said, "Did I hurt you? Do something wrong?"

"Not at all. But you nearly ended things before they began. Not so fast, love. We have all night."

* * *

They spent the remainder of the night caught up in each other's desires. With him reaching out for her and her reaching back for him. Things were so easy this time, as if they'd been made especially to fit together. And maybe they had been.

In the early hours of morning, he tortured her by kissing his way down her body until she shattered. Then he spent time nuzzling the inside of her thighs until he had her gasping and ready once again.

He lifted his head and grinned up at her. "You're the best. One more time for me, darling."

"For you," she murmured as he slid into place inside her waiting body.

"Only for me."

The dark possession in his words thrilled her beyond measure. But before she could let the sentiment sink in, his thrusts became frenzied and the momentum of the moment carried her away.

After they'd climaxed together, he held her in his arms. She cried with the sheer depth of her feelings, and discovered, to her amazement, that Colin's eyes were tearing up, too. Locking her arms around his neck, she let him rock her into a sound and peaceful sleep.

As the dawn broke, Maggie sat in her kitchen, feeding Emma a bottle and listening as the water in the pipes told her Colin was up and in the shower. Outside, a hiss of sleet slapped against the windowpanes. The overrunning had turned icy during the night.

What should she do first? Several things competed for priority in her mind. She'd never gotten around to telling Colin that she loved him last night. But by the light of day, saying that didn't seem quite appropriate. She *would* tell him she loved him someday. Just not today.

Emma made a cooing noise and captured her attention. Yes, first things first. She had to decide what would be her best move to protect the baby from whatever evil was stalking her. Maggie needed to contact her *abuela* for advice.

"Come on, baby doll." She stood, bringing both Emma and the bottle with her. "Let's go into the office. Uncle Colin will find us there when he needs us."

By the time Colin found Maggie, he had himself worked into a frenzy. "Where the hell have you two been? I've been searching all over."

Startled, she glanced down at Emma playing on the floor. "Um, we're right here. Did you need something?"

He couldn't blurt out everything he desired all at once. He wasn't sure of it all himself. Besides, other important matters must be taken care of first. Things like safety and security. Nothing could happen to these two now. Nothing. He would die before he let either the leader of a drug cartel or a black witch hurt them.

But Maggie was not going to see things his way. She always thought she could protect herself from everything. This time, he could not let her use pride to keep him from doing what was right. After all, that was something he knew all about and had let stand in his way for most of his life. He steeled himself for an argument.

"I've called my mother. It was easier than I thought." Easier when he'd realized he needed something from her so desperately. "She's flying in and should be here soon. She'll be taking Emma."

Maggie paled. "Taking Emma? Oh, my God, Colin, no!"

Chapter 12

Maggie wondered if her life would play out before her eyes, the way they said it did when you were dying. Surely, she was dying. Why else would her heart stop beating and her vision start to fade?

"*Both* you and the baby are going with my mother to get away from danger," Colin said with authority. "It's too dangerous for you to stay here. I've asked Mum to fly into Texas and notify me when she arrives."

The air whooshed from Maggie's lungs. "I'm not going to leave. This is my home. I grew up here. I'm safer on the Delgado Ranch than I am anywhere else on earth."

Colin glared at her for a second. Then it hit her.

"You called your mother! Oh, Colin, that's wonderful. How did she take the news about John?"

"She was as weird as ever," he said with a disgusted

sigh. "She said she'd already known in her heart about John and had been waiting for my call."

Maggie's pounding heart began to steady. "That doesn't sound weird to me. If anything happened to Emma, I'm sure, somehow, I would know."

She stood and went up on tiptoes to give Colin a kiss. "You were worried about us. That's sweet."

More than just sweet, it gave her hope that there might be a future for them. But she couldn't say anything about their tomorrows just yet. They still had to get past a difficult today.

"Nothing can happen to either one of you," he told her. "If you refuse to be safe, I can't force you to leave. But I'll take the baby out of harm's way, then come back to protect you."

Judging from his protective stance and the fierce warrior look in his eyes, he'd already come to love his niece. Maggie had so hoped that would happen. Now she had only to convince him that she was the best one to raise the child.

"Calm down, please," she said softly. "We're not going to take the baby anywhere in this sleet. Maybe the weather will clear up by tomorrow."

He frowned. "It will snow by tomorrow."

"What makes you say that?" She held in a chuckle. "It almost never snows in South Texas. This overrunning rain is coming out of the southwest. It might be nasty stuff, but a southwest wind means it can't snow."

"It'll snow. I feel the change in my bones."

Maggie decided not to argue about anything so crazy, so she shrugged and changed the subject. "I've just spent the last hour e-mailing with my grandmother. She happens to agree with you that the danger is getting closer. But we're battling a man who uses black magic. Running will not work in this case. He'll find the baby, wherever she goes."

Colin took a breath and plopped himself down in an easy chair next to her desk. "So what then? Do we use our own black magic to fight fire with fire?"

Maggie shook her head, but smiled at him. She'd noticed he hadn't denied the possibility that her grandmother's analysis was true. Or that Maggie had the ability to fight black magic. Maybe he was beginning to believe the truth about her and her family. It might be another good sign in favor of their having a future together.

"My grandmother will certainly lend her white magic to our cause, but from a distance," she said. "We don't need black magic to fight the evil or to protect Emma from the *brujo*. We only have to be smarter than he is. And sneakier."

Colin's eyes glittered. and then he smiled back at her. "You know, love, I believe you can do whatever you set your mind to do. So…how do we proceed?"

"We're going to use what we learned from that assault last night. I have a plan."

Governor Garcia set aside the note he was reading and casually picked up a piece of toast. Sitting across the breakfast table from the man, the *jefe* understood why the atmosphere in the room had changed, even though no words had been spoken.

The governor knew. That note must have been the last piece in the puzzle of what had happened to the governor's daughter. If the *jefe* was going to live through the next few minutes, he would have to act quickly.

"Was that message bad news, *Patrón?*" The *jefe* felt

the sweat beading in the creases of his neck. He fingered the heavy gold chain partially hidden under his shirt's collar.

"Indeed it was bad news, Hector. The worst news imaginable."

The governor had called him by his proper name. The *jefe* could only imagine what that meant. He stared at the other man in silence, afraid to open his mouth.

"My daughter *es muerto*." The governor sat back in his chair, the toast completely forgotten. "When I first learned that she had run away with Juan, I swore to find that traitor and kill him. It seems someone has taken that pleasure from my hands."

The *jefe* didn't like the look in the governor's eyes. Black as coal, they appeared as deadly as a snake's, while they drilled deadly intent into the *jefe's* own.

"But in the taking of a traitor's life, my precious daughter was also sacrificed," the governor continued. "Do you know how that makes me feel, Hector, or what that would have meant to my dead wife? It will also mean much to the man who issued those orders. Do you see?"

The *jefe* shook his head slowly. He felt as if he were already choking on his own vomit, gasping out his last breath. His fingers slipped around his specially designed amulet, the one secretly secured to the golden chain.

"No?" The smile on the governor's lips made the *jefe's* blood run cold. "Ah, but you will."

The next thing that *jefe* knew he was staring down the huge barrel of a gun. "Stand up, Hector. I have special plans for you."

"Wait, *Patrón*. Wait." The *jefe* got to his feet, but had to support himself by leaning against the table. "You have a granddaughter. I know where the child is. Kill me and you will never know."

At those words, the governor's gun barrel wavered to the left and the *jefe* figured he would never have a better chance to help himself. He lifted his devil amulet, loaded with evil magic, from around his neck and flashed it toward the governor.

Instantly a dark shadow moved across the governor's face and the man's fingers loosened on his gun. The *jefe* grabbed a sharp knife from the table and dived toward the governor's chest.

With one swift and deadly thrust, the *jefe* snuffed out the threat to his life. The formerly invulnerable governor would never make another move to harm him or anyone else.

Not totally free yet, the *jefe* starred down at the glassy-eyed death mask of the once very powerful man and wondered if he himself had enough power left to escape the governor's men, as well as his for-midable political comrades. Governor Garcia's men ran this state and much of Mexico, and every one of them would like to be the one to take down the governor's killer.

The *jefe* had his own men and comrades—and plenty of money for *la mordida*. Still, he knew his life would be worthless if he stayed in Mexico now.

He needed to head for the border right away. As it happened, there was a place on the other side where he had unfinished business. And people on his payroll to help him cross.

Perhaps even the child there would still be useful to him. Yes, that was definitely the direction he should run.

* * *

It had been more than twenty-four hours since Maggie had concocted her plan, Colin reflected, as he drove the SUV down the icy streets of Zavala Springs. Twenty-four hours full of arguments for and against each point of view, of recruiting assistance from family and friends, and of biding their time waiting with pleasurable hours in bed.

Extremely pleasurable hours. Colin shook off the haze of lust that always surrounded him when he thought of his time spent making love with Maggie. He had a feeling their pleasant interludes were almost over. But he was trying to convince himself that would only be for the best. Another few nights spent in her bed, and he might never be able to leave. Leaving in the end had always been nonnegotiable, in his head, if not in his heart. As much as he admired her, certainly desired her, and…yes…cared for her, their differing backgrounds and Maggie's uniqueness would make a future with her impossible.

Hadn't he seen how badly something like that had worked out during his childhood? Hadn't he promised himself that he would never become involved with anyone from such a different world? He had done so, and he planned to stick with his instincts. They'd served him well, so far in this life.

For now, Colin was determined to see his brother's murderer pay for his crimes. And to assure himself that Maggie and Emma were safe from any danger. Their peril was all his fault, after all. He had brought the evil straight to their door.

Maggie's plan to save Emma was sound, as far as it went. But Colin had a secret plan of his own. A plan to see to their safety for good.

He pulled up in front of the sheriff's station and stepped out into the frigid air. Looking up at large white flakes falling softly from a dove-gray sky, he hunched down in his jacket and snorted. So it never snowed in south Texas? Today it would. And that snow would be the perfect accompaniment to Maggie's plan.

As Colin headed for the door, he comforted himself with thinking how sure he was of his target. Only one man in town could be responsible for everything that had transpired so far. The one man who must be secretly on the drug lord's payroll.

Opening the glass front door and stomping the slush off his boots, Colin glanced around the station until he spotted him. The man's face, though a few years older in appearance, matched perfectly with the pictures Colin and Maggie had found on the Internet yesterday. Pictures taken long ago of Deputy Gutierrez with his Mexican national mother and sister. At the time they had been visiting the United States for his U.S. Border Patrol swearing in. It had taken Maggie hours of research, but she'd matched the names of his mother and sister to the names of several Mexican women killed last year in a gun battle with the international strike team at the drug lord's hacienda. "Collateral damage" was how the article had described the women's fate.

He and Maggie had put two and two together. Deputy Gutierrez was their best pick for the bad guy, at least on this side of the border. Revenge was a nasty motive for murder. Colin was quite familiar with that same emotion. He headed in the deputy's direction.

"*Hola*, Señor Fairfax," the deputy called out as he came near. "What can I do for you? I'm afraid you've missed Sheriff Ochoa again today. He has traveled to Austin for an important meeting."

Recruiting the sheriff's help had not been part of Maggie's plan, because they weren't sure of his loyalties. Regardless of the circumstances, the plan would still work. It had to.

"You can take my statement as easily as the sheriff, Deputy." Colin shrugged off his jacket and waited for an invitation to sit.

"Statement? Have you committed some crime? Or maybe you witnessed one?" The deputy stood still as he studied Colin.

"Look, are you going to take down my story, or do I have to drive to Austin to get the sheriff's attention?" Colin raised his voice just loudly enough to make the other people in the room turn to see what was going on.

"*Sí, señor.*" The deputy moved quickly then, and led him to a private conference room. "Please make yourself comfortable and let me know how I might help you."

"I don't want to be comfortable," Colin roared as he turned on the deputy. "Someone tried to kidnap my niece the other night, and they roughed up Ms. Ryan in the attempt. I demand that the sheriff's department provide better security for the citizens of Zavala Springs. People are not safe in their own homes!"

"Kidnapping! Why didn't you call the sheriff immediately? Was anyone injured? Is the child safe?"

We didn't call because we were afraid of inviting the fox right into the henhouse. Colin kept his wry remarks to himself, and schooled his features to remain sober as he continued with the charade.

"Everyone is all right. The baby is perfectly sound, though Ms. Ryan has a slight sprain. But she didn't wish to bother the sheriff when it would be only her word. No one witnessed the attack."

He lasered his eyes at the deputy. "But I am not so careful about your U.S. legal regulations and expectations," he continued in an even louder voice. "I demand that your department protect Ms. Ryan, as she doesn't want to leave her home. But I myself have no wish to wait around for a next time."

Colin lowered his voice and added a deadly rasp. "My intention is to remove my niece from the danger zone. This afternoon I'm driving the baby to San Antonio. And good riddance to your whole country."

The deputy paled, but to his credit he kept a professional attitude. "Tomorrow we will interview Ms. Ryan, *señor.* And the sheriff's department will provide whatever protection she wishes. If you want to leave, of course you can. But may I caution that bad weather is forecasted? A freak snowstorm is headed our way. The roads will be dangerous. Perhaps you should wait until tomorrow or the next day?"

"Not at all," Colin said with a nonchalant wave. "I'm British, and I'm not afraid of a few snowflakes. On our way out of your jurisdiction, I intend to make one quick stop at the spot where my brother was killed, so that my niece and I can pay our last respects. After that, you will have seen the last of us."

Was it his imagination or did the deputy seem to be a captive audience all of a sudden?

"But," he added forcefully, "*do* expect to hear from my solicitors concerning John's murder. Advise the sheriff to watch for their letter."

With that last dig, he turned and stormed out of the sheriff's station. Totally satisfied that he had put on a good show, he was sure Maggie's plan would produce the desired effects. Then, perhaps he would add a surprise or two of his own.

The winds were fierce and the snow was coming down in huge clumps. How on earth had Colin known a blue norther had been headed their way a full two days before the weatherman even predicted one?

Maggie shrugged, unwilling to think about that right now, and pulled her old felt cowboy hat lower on her forehead. Moving down the porch steps, she shrank into her heavy coat and pulled the lapels together with her hands.

Showtime.

But with the last step, her boots were buried in a half foot of slush and new snow, and she wondered if their show had any chance of being observed. For certain, if she didn't have to be out here in this ridiculously cold weather, she would be upstairs, safe and warm in her bed.

Colin preceded her and Seguro down the walk, but he was going slow as he carried the precious cargo. He was only two or three steps ahead of her, but she almost lost sight of him in the swirling flakes.

Time for her to start her act. But goodness only knew if the right person would be watching.

"Colin, damn it! Wait up!"

Maggie flung herself down the slippery walk until she reached him. His back was to her, as he unlocked the SUV and opened the back door with one hand. Safe in the crook of his other arm rested the bundled-up little girl.

Beating her fists against his broad back, Maggie made sure her voice was raised. "Don't take Emma away from me. Please, Colin. You know it will kill me to lose her."

He quickly set the blanket-bundled baby doll in her car seat and latched her in tight. Then he turned around.

"No more discussion. The decision is made. The child is going with me to somewhere she'll be safe. Go back into the house before you catch your death. We're leaving."

The look in his eyes turned dark and serious. Suddenly, this whole situation didn't seem so much like an act as it did like one of her nightmares. Maggie started to tremble.

She made a grab for him and caught hold of a piece of his coat. "I've changed my mind. You can't borrow the SUV. Don't leave me. Stay. I...*need* you."

Colin jerked away from her grasp and opened the driver's door. He reached in, turned on the motor and the heater then turned around to face her again.

"Thank you for your kind hospitality. I'll leave the SUV at the San Antonio airport where you can pick it up. If you wish to see Emma in the future, please contact my mother."

"But...but...wait!" She threw her arms around his neck and moved in close. Too close for anyone else to hear. "I love you, Colin. Please take care of yourself. I'll see you soon."

He peeled her arms from around his neck and put one foot inside the car while snow drifted around his other ankle. She expected that he would bend low enough to whisper some word or give her a quick kiss. Especially now that she had admitted her love.

But that's not what happened. Colin reached around with his forearm and swiped the snow off the windshield.

After the glass was cleaned, he slid down all the way into the seat behind the steering wheel, without a word.

Putting the SUV into gear, he stepped on the brake and faced her. "Forget me, Mags. It never would have worked between us anyway."

Oh, God. Her heart was breaking. But this couldn't be for real. His leaving was all part of the act, wasn't it?

Colin spoke to the dog, then reached over and pulled his door almost all the way shut. "Goodbye, Mags."

Stunned, Maggie wiped snow from her eyes and watched as he slammed his door and drove away.

Chapter 13

Standing perfectly still, Maggie held her breath until she thought her lungs would burst. She watched Colin drive down the street and turn the corner onto the main road. Then he was gone.

Something about the way he'd left didn't feel right. The look in his eyes had bothered her. It was almost as if… No, that expression couldn't have been what she'd thought. It looked for all the world like the despair you might see in the eyes of a man going off on a mission who was sure he would never come back.

No possibility of that, though. She had made an excellent plan. All he had to do was go along with it and the bad guy would be captured. But still, his look…

She stomped around in her yard for the next fifteen minutes, sticking to her end of the plan. Dodging snowflakes and ignoring her reservations about Colin, she marveled at the unusual snowstorm. The accumulation of snow wouldn't last long. By tomorrow the sun would be shining and the thermometer would register well over the freezing mark. Such was the changeable weather in this part of Texas, she knew. Yet, wasn't it an interesting development?

Seguro followed her back and forth, staying right by her side as she circled around the house and bided her time. He bit at the snowflakes and chased them in the wind. Finally the dog nudged her hand and whined.

"Yes, all right, Seguro. It should be okay now." Maggie went around to the backyard and she and the dog snuck through the hedgerow, heading for the neighbor's house.

Lara was waiting for her, watching out of her kitchen window. She opened the door just as Maggie and the dog stepped up on the porch, and then shut it quickly behind them.

"Do you suppose anyone is still around and watching? Was I spotted?" Maggie asked as she took off her boots and left them just inside the kitchen door.

Lara was busy toweling off Seguro's paws. "If you were, no one will think anything of it. For the last ten years you've landed over here every time you needed to talk. We're old friends and everyone knows it."

Maggie nodded and went straight for the high chair and baby Emma. "I hope so. That's what this charade was all about."

She pulled Emma up and into her arms, snuggling her close. Emma reared back and reached out to touch a snowflake still attached to Maggie's coat. It melted at her touch and the baby grinned and pointed.

"Yes, it's called snow. But you won't see that very often in Zavala Springs. Are you ready to go, Emma?"

"She just needs her coat," Lara answered for the baby. "Her diaper bag and duffel are already packed into the Jeep. How long do you think she will have to stay away?"

Maggie knew Lara would miss seeing Emma every day, but removing the child from danger was the most important thing. "I hope for only a few days at most. If my plan works, as soon as Colin crosses the county line, that international task force will swoop down and capture whoever is following him. We're guessing it'll turn out to be the deputy sheriff in the end."

Trying to hide her growing anxiety, Maggie continued calmly, "After we've got the bad guy in custody, the task force wants Colin to go to Mexico to tell authorities there what happened to his brother and about the connection to the deputy and the drug lord. They're hoping to have the drug lord in custody by then."

"That sounds dangerous for Colin."

"It shouldn't be. I'll make sure he's protected by magic before he leaves, and Abuela Lupe can keep an eye on him while he's in Mexico. And of course, he will be guarded by the task force and several U.S. and British politicians. That ought to keep him safe enough."

If Maggie had thought for a moment that he wouldn't be safe, she never would've encouraged him to carry out his end of the plan. Or if he felt he had to, she would've gone with him. After all, this had been *her* plan.

Lara helped her with Emma's coat and disguise. If anyone was still watching, it would just seem that Maggie was taking a pile of towels and clothes out to the Jeep behind Lara's house. The baby giggled as they put her into the cardboard box, lightly covered her with blankets and stuffed towels in between her and the box's sides.

"You're sure you don't need my help to drive?" Lara asked after everything was ready.

Maggie shook her head. "No, thanks. My father is prepared. He'll have men on the road to watch out for us."

"I still don't understand why you're going to your father's ranch house rather than one of your brothers' houses. You and your father haven't been particularly close over the last fifteen years."

Lara was right, but Maggie had thought this all through carefully. "Anyone who's been watching me for the last week or so would easily think to look for me at both Josh's and Ethan's places. I take Emma there all the time, but how long has it been since I've been to my father's house? Emma has never even been there. We don't want to make things any easier for the bad guys."

Maggie's voice wound down with her nerves. "Besides, my father has the men and the firepower to protect Emma that my brothers don't."

Lara nodded as she helped carry the box with Emma out to the Jeep. Lara blocked the view with her body as Maggie lifted Emma out and buckled her safely into a borrowed car seat in the back. "Take care. And be careful." She waved at Seguro, and he jumped in the back and dropped quietly to the floor.

Maggie intended to do much more than be careful. She swore nothing would go wrong with her plan.

On foot and alone on the Texas range, Colin lifted his head at the noise from a motorized vehicle and searched the horizon. The rolling landscape, currently bathed in a half foot of snow, should be easy enough to scan, even in the growing twilight and with the naked eye. But the natural nooks and crannies in this part of the western United States were making his investigation of the landscape difficult.

Rock outcroppings and clumps of trees kept him from discerning the direction of the sound. Trying to judge the kind of vehicle by the motor's high-pitched whine, he knew it had to be some kind of motorcycle, snowmobile or perhaps an ATV.

At that moment, the whining noise in the distance split into many distinct sounds. Not just one assailant then, but several.

He breathed out a heavy sigh and tried to clear his head. When he'd first devised his secret plan to confront the bad guy away from Maggie and without any of her family's help, he had thought the confrontation would be easy. Just a personal showdown between himself and Deputy Gutierrez. Emma and Maggie would be safe with her father by the time he faced the deputy, so he'd felt he needn't worry about them.

Colin still believed he stood a fifty-fifty chance of ending up victorious against the man who'd taken John's life. Man against man. Colin had faced tougher odds many times and lived to talk about them. And he felt strongly that he must do this alone. It was his responsibility to John to take down his murderer.

But when Colin had stopped Maggie's SUV at the ravine crossing where John and his wife died and then took one of Josh's carbines from its hiding place in Emma's car seat, he hadn't counted on what happened next. After he'd secreted himself behind a large tree to wait for the deputy, an entire army of men appeared out of the landscape.

The assailants were bent on kidnapping Emma and killing him. It had been everything he could manage, using every guerilla tactic he'd ever learned, to escape the ambush.

By now he was sure the assailants had guessed that the whole story of his transporting Emma had been a ruse. But apparently he was still a significant enough target to keep them searching through the sage and cactus into the night.

He'd long ago figured out that the Mexican drug lord who'd ordered John murdered was determined to have him killed, too, rather than let him continue asking questions. But the time for questions was now over and Colin had thought that it might mean he would be in the clear. Apparently not. So, he must have gotten one too many right answers.

Tension arched through the night, as an ATV with oversize wheels appeared out of the trees and whizzed across the flat, heading straight for him. He dived for cover. Wishing he had something far superior in fire-power than the carbine, he sited the weapon and waited until the attacker was close enough.

Rifle fire suddenly blasted in his direction when a second ATV followed the first out of the night. Colin got a shot off and watched as the dark silhouette of the first driver went flying off his ride. But the second ATV was still coming, and by then a third and fourth had appeared, too.

He was outgunned again. Without giving it a lot of thought, he jumped up and plowed through the snow, running full out for the idling and driverless ATV. Firing off a few rounds from his lever-action rifle to hold them off, Colin grunted with the effort of getting there before the second man could close in.

Bullets creased a mesquite tree five feet from Colin's

head, just as he threw himself into the seat and fumbled with the controls. The ATV was similar in design to those he'd ridden in the 'Stan. He gunned it and felt the powerful engine buck under him.

Not having a clue about directions out here on the range, Colin just took off in a zigzag pattern, trying to outrun his attackers. The light was almost gone now, but he opened it up full throttle and kept the headlights turned off.

Behind him he could hear yelling over the engine sounds and imagined the attackers were trying to corner his machine or run him into a ravine. Things were looking bleak.

As he took a course too close to the trees, branches slashed at his face. Running this blind was stupid, but he didn't have the luxury of stopping to take a stand. Not while the danger was so close on his heels.

With his heart jackhammering against his ribs, Colin was growing desperate. Outrunning them was impossible. He swerved around a rock outcropping that he'd only spotted at the last moment. Gravel spewed out from under his tires as he guided the ATV down a wash on the other side.

Now he was at last entering terrain where he could use the evasive tactics he'd been so good at in the Afghan mountains. If only twilight would hold on just a little longer. In pitch darkness, he would need to go to ground. Find a good hiding place and lay low until he could figure out a better plan. He wished he still had his regimental tactical equipment. Night vision glasses would come in handy about now.

He heard the revving motors of the vehicles in pursuit as they strained to take the wash and stay upright at the same time. Halfway up the side of the deepening wash, Colin shot ahead into a gap. His ATV tilted until he was riding on one set of wheels, but he flew on into the night.

Far enough ahead of them now, Colin spotted his potential salvation. A big ravine widening out dead ahead.

He slowed to gauge his best track and then twisted the gas control, bringing life back into the idling ATV under him. With one bone-jarring jolt, he took to the air and landed roughly on the far side of the ravine.

He felt a bit safer, inched back on the throttle and listened. The other engine sounds had grown distant. Distant enough to put a new maneuver into motion. Colin found a good spot farther down on the rim of the ravine, where three boulders stood together.

There he wedged his ATV into a tight crevice, put it into neutral, and removed his handkerchief from his coat pocket. He wound the material square around the throttle, then tightened it down until the engine whined fruitlessly all by itself.

Grabbing up the carbine, Colin went straight to the edge of the ravine and jumped, rolling into a tight ball as his body careened down the snow-covered side. At the bottom, he gave thanks for being lucky and picking a spot with no boulders or hidden drop-offs. Now he was on foot and needed to get away from this spot fast.

Dusting snow off his jacket, he started out, staying in the shadow of the ravine's overhang, and hoping to keep his footprints to a minimum on the rocks. In the distance he could hear the other ATVs following along the rim.

By the time he spotted the first star shining brightly in a clear sky, all motor sounds were far in the distance. Still, it was too cold and too dangerous, in territory he didn't recognize, to stay outside and keep going for much longer. He looked up, noticing that the rim's overhang stuck out farther than before, and realized the ravine had grown deeper and narrower. Narrow enough here that an ATV wouldn't be able to negotiate at the bottom. He was betting this was a dry wash and it might be a perfect place to tunnel in while he devised a new plan for getting to Gutierrez.

Maggie slowed the Jeep at Zavala Ravine, where John and his wife had been killed, but she couldn't make out anything in the darkness. Emma fussed in her car seat in the back. The baby wasn't used to riding in this vehicle that belonged to her grandfather, and she needed to be home in bed. Seguro whined from his spot on the floor of the backseat.

"We have to find Colin," she murmured to both the baby and the dog. "He must be in trouble."

On her way to her father's ranch, Maggie had used one of his satellite phones to check with Marshall Sam Dodd, who was still waiting up ahead with the international task force. Colin had never made it that far. Maggie was guessing that he'd stopped here for some reason, though it wasn't a part of her plan for him to stop anywhere on the road.

The snow let up for the moment, and a shaft of bright moonlight filtered down through the trees around the ravine. She spotted her SUV, pulled way off the road and seemingly abandoned, with its doors standing ajar.

Oh my God!

Maggie carefully guided the Jeep onto the shoulder, put it into park, but left the motor running. Staying in the safety of the vehicle, she placed a call to her father and explained her predicament. Not knowing how much trouble Colin might be in, she asked her father to send his men as backup. Delgado ranch hands knew every inch of this landscape, and they would come to her and Colin's aid with ATVs, horses and guns.

She extracted a promise of help from her father and then put in a call to the international task force. She wasn't sure if they had the manpower to spread out over a hundred square miles of range land, so she'd asked them to coordinate with her father's men.

Once that was done, she slid the phone back into her jacket pocket, but she couldn't help feeling she should do something more. Urgently needing to drive Emma to safety at the Delgado Ranch, Maggie still couldn't just leave Colin out on a range he didn't know anything about, at the mercy of who knew what evil.

Checking in her rearview mirror for traffic and finding none at this late hour on this isolated stretch of road, she reached into her backpack and extracted her grandmother's crystal. The least she could do before driving away was to find Colin's whereabouts. Then she would notify the task force of what she'd learned. She could only hope that they would pay attention and not ignore the help provided from her witchcraft.

She flipped on the dashboard lights and gazed into the cloudy crystal. Hazy images deep inside the glass began to swirl, then clear. For one instant she caught sight of Colin. But it was enough to tell her he was alive and seemed to be encased in snow. The crystal warmed in her hand and she felt he was okay for the moment, and knew that he was safe in a place she recognized.

Seguro growled, low and fierce in his throat.

"Oh, he's okay, Seguro. It looks to me like he's down in Wrangler's dry wash, but we need to—"

The crystal suddenly went dark as the Jeep's doors were jerked open.

"Out, bitch!"

Maggie gasped and dropped the crystal on the floor mat. Roughly dragged from the driver's seat by a pair of big hands, she screamed and fought to get to Emma. She could hear Seguro snapping and growling in defense of the child, but there was nothing she could do to help.

Overpowered, she kicked and struggled until someone hit her across the face. She fell to her knees just as Emma let out a shriek. Maggie couldn't see what was going on, but she heard the dog and knew he was fighting his best.

"Ow! Damned dog. Shoot him!" A familiar male voice growled out orders in Spanish.

She knew the voice belonged to Deputy Gutierrez and worry about Emma made her light-headed. "The baby! Don't hurt her!"

"Shut up." Gutierrez pulled her to her feet by the hair and shouted over Seguro's barking. "And shut that damned dog up for good. Get him!"

The pain had her seeing stars, but she came up swinging. Until…a shot rang out above the fray. The next sound she heard was a dog's yip of pain—and then silence reigned.

Seguro!

An hour later, Colin sat cross-legged inside a half snow cave, half rock crevice, listening intently for any sound. He hadn't heard the ATV engine noises in quite a while, and he was temporarily out of the elements and staying dry. But he was freezing his tail off by not moving. Even the water in the bottle had frozen solid.

His eyes had become accustomed to the dark and he needed to get going. Gutierrez was out there somewhere, he was sure, and Colin was more determined than ever to take him down.

A low growl echoed through the air. Colin wondered if it could be his stomach protesting missing a couple of meals. But when it happened again, he knew it hadn't been him. He reached for the carbine and sat perfectly still.

Soon he heard a snuffling sound and then something that sounded like paws clawing at the rocks and snow he'd used to cover the entrance to his cave. Not a human sound, he wondered what kind of creature was coming through the snow to attack him. Bears weren't known in this part of Texas, he didn't think. And certainly not at this time of year.

He leveled his weapon and the tiny beam of his small flashlight at the entrance and held his breath. Rock and snow shifted as the tiny opening grew. But instead of another growl, the next sound he heard was a distinct whine. Wracking his brain, he couldn't come up with what sort of wild animal would make such a noise.

When a dog's muzzle finally pushed through into his cave, Colin understood everything. His assailants had used tracking dogs to ferret him out into the open. His finger tightened down on the trigger.

"Woof!" Something in that dog's muffled greeting told Colin this encounter would not be what he'd anticipated.

In another second, Seguro inched through the opening just as Colin let up on the trigger. "Hello, dog. Where's your mistress?"

Damn Maggie anyway. She must have used her magic to find him. Colin felt the fury rolling over him. She had no business interfering. This was his mission and obligation. Not hers.

But as Seguro stuffed his whole body into the small crevice, a shaft from Colin's flashlight beam fell over the dog's back. Colin spotted the blood in an instant, and a sudden, deadly dread took his breath away.

"You're hurt. What's happened? Where's Maggie, Seguro?"

The dog only whined and put his nose up against Colin's hand. "All right." It seemed clear that the witch dog wanted to go with him. "We'll look for her together."

Emma and Maggie had better be okay. They just had to be—or his life might as well end right here.

Chapter 14

Maggie shivered and tried to stop trembling. Balancing on the back of an ATV that was going at top speed over the snowy, rock-filled range, with her hands tied behind her back and tape over her mouth, was not the easiest thing she had ever done. It wasn't the frigid temperature or the wild ride giving her the shakes, though she knew whizzing through the darkness behind a man who clearly didn't know where he was going would probably not end well for either of them.

None of that mattered. Emma's welfare mattered. These cretins had pulled Emma's car seat out of the Jeep and tied it, with the baby still inside, onto the back of one of the other ATVs. Maggie had begged them to at least put the baby blanket over the infant's face to keep her from freezing, which, thankfully, they did at the last minute.

Apparently, they wanted to keep Emma alive. That was Maggie's main objective as well. But staying out in the cold for very much longer could be deadly for a baby. Maggie trembled at the thought.

With every bump and slide of the ATV, Maggie held her breath. But along with every jolt she felt the protection charm bouncing at her throat, and she remembered that Emma was also protected by her own amulet.

The notion kept Maggie from being hysterical, but she sure wished she knew a little bit more about black magic. If she did, she would be throwing hexes and curses at Deputy Gutierrez until he ended this craziness and let them go.

Just then, Gutierrez slowed the ATV and came to a stop. The other ATVs pulled up behind him while his machine continued to rumble in neutral. Maggie wondered what was wrong while she tried to get a glimpse of Emma.

"*Qué pasó?*" One of the other men echoed her sentiments.

Gutierrez ignored the question as he pulled a GPS unit from his coat pocket. He shook the thing and stared at the night sky.

Maggie's confidence in his ability to find his way across the range sunk to a new low. Wherever he thought they were headed, they needed to arrive there soon. For the baby's sake. She mumbled under the tape across her mouth, trying to say she would be glad to guide them if it would get them there sooner—and safer.

"Be still!" Gutierrez pinched her arm.

He turned his attention to the lighted dial on his wristwatch and cursed. "Being late is not an option."

Swinging around in his seat, he spoke to the other two men on their ATVs. "You were with the *jefe* and helped him cross the border. How did you find that damned line shack in the dark?"

"The *jefe* is a powerful *brujo*," one of the men said over the engine noise. "Darkness is his friend."

Maggie felt fear like an icicle down her spine. The black witch was already here on the Delgado Ranch. Here, and waiting for them.

The silence was getting to Colin. He and Seguro had been making good time on foot, and they had probably covered a couple of miles over the last half hour. But things were too quiet.

As they rounded a thick stand of mesquite, the dog whined and began crawling ahead on his belly. Colin didn't need to speak dog in order to understand the sudden need to stay low. He bent at the waist and knees and kept as small a profile as possible without going to his hands and knees.

Then he heard noises nearby that he immediately recognized. The muffled whispers through the night air did not seem ominous at all. Indeed, he'd heard these same sounds many times before and knew at once the quiet snuffling and soft rustling of horses at rest for the night.

His eyes focused in on an isolated and darkened corral dead ahead. He didn't stop to count them, but he thought there must be about fifteen head within the fence. Wondering what this place was and why Seguro had led him here, he moved in for a closer inspection.

No one seemed to be around. He couldn't spot any dwellings or barns nearby. But just as he was about to scout out a little farther, suddenly the entire surrounding area came alive with blinding light.

"Hold it, son. Drop the carbine and put your hands where I can see them."

Colin halted, lowered the weapon to the ground and raised his arms above his head. When he slowly turned toward the voice, he realized that the lights were headlights, coming from about a dozen ATVs spread in a circle around the corral. This was a trap, and Seguro had led him right into it.

Bloody hell.

"Colin Fairfax, is that you?" A different male voice rang out from the darkness beyond the light. With no trace of a Latin accent, this voice was still one he'd heard before but couldn't place.

"Yes. Who's there?" He lowered his hands and tried to shield his eyes from the light.

"Douse the lights." With that order, the blackness of the night returned.

It took a few seconds for his eyes to adjust to the dark again. When they did, he saw Maggie's brother Ethan and her father Brody walking up to him. He took a quick, calming breath.

"Where's Maggie?" Her welfare was all he cared about at the moment.

"Maggie and Emma have been kidnapped," Brody Ryan said with a snarl. "Taken right out of my Jeep on a public road."

"Emma? The baby's gone, too?"

"Danged right. And we figured you were either dead or in the same spot with them. Glad to find you alive, son."

Blinded now with fear for the two females he loved

more than anything, Colin could barely speak. "We have to find them. They could be anywhere. We have to—"

"Stay calm. We don't know their condition, but we know exactly where they are."

"Where? How?"

"They're headed this way," Ethan told him. "Maggie has one of the Delgado's satellite phones in her pocket. All our phones have GPS units, and we've been picking up her signal since they left the highway."

"Dang fools seem to be lost," Brody added. "They've been wandering around the range like stinking drunks. But we've got a copter in the air keeping an eye on them from above."

"What about the roads? How can you be sure Maggie and the baby are actually with the satellite phone?"

Brody gave him a quick nod to show his approval of a good question. "That Marshall Dodd fellow and his buddies have the roads covered. When you failed to show up, they closed the highways in all directions."

Colin took another breath and straightened his shoulders. "Why do you believe the kidnappers are coming here?"

"It makes sense. If they wanted to cross the border or just hide out on the range, they'd be smart to get off the motorized vehicles and on to horseback. Someone must have figured out the Delgado keeps a few animals corralled here for the winter."

Colin swung in a complete circle then turned back to Brody. "Who feeds and checks on these animals during the winter? Isn't this a long way out in the middle of nowhere?"

Brody looked at him with a strange expression on his face. "Our hands make regular rounds all year long. We ride the fences and check stock tanks no matter the weather. There's a line shack about a quarter mile away in case anyone needs shelter for the night." He flicked his thumb behind him. "That direction."

"What if Maggie and Emma's captors are going there instead of coming here?"

Brody thought about it for a second. "Tell you what, we'll send a couple of—"

The buzz from a vibrating mobile phone took everyone's attention as Brody pulled one from his pocket and answered it. Without saying anything, he pocketed the phone.

"No time now," he told Colin. "The copter pilot says the three ATVs are definitely heading here. And they'll be arriving within minutes."

Brody ordered everyone back into hiding. All hands scattered noiselessly.

Colin reached out his hand and stopped Brody before he, too, could disappear. "I need to do something to help. Give me a rifle."

Brody shook his head. "Not such a good idea, son. I don't want you—"

Ethan came back into the clearing carrying a sniper rifle with a night scope and handed it to Colin. "I Googled you, *Major* Fairfax. Imagine my surprise to find a world-class marksman like yourself on our lowly ranch. And then I thought we might need an expert backup shot like you tonight, so I brought the appropriate weapon. Why don't you move off behind those trees, where you can have a good sight line, and let us see what we can do first to save Maggie and Emma without any shooting?"

Hefting the rifle, Colin did as he was instructed and

slid into place behind a six-foot cactus. Seguro had disappeared off into the night when Ethan and Brody had appeared. Colin hoped the dog was okay and would stay quiet like everyone else during this operation. He wasn't completely sure of the Ryans' plan, but he stood ready to take any measure necessary to save Maggie and Emma.

Colin barely made it into hiding when the sounds of ATV motors split the air. Soon three headlights beamed through the darkness, coming in fast.

With a rush of noise and bluster, the ATVs roared into the clearing and shut down. Colin's heart nearly shut down, too, when he saw Deputy Gutierrez pulling Maggie off the back of his ATV. Through his scope, he also spotted an infant's car seat on the back of another ATV. But the man driving her vehicle did not dismount. He stayed where he was, apparently waiting for orders.

"We're switching to horses here," Gutierrez told his men. "*El Jefe* is waiting close by with tack."

The deputy ripped tape off Maggie's mouth. "Keep quiet, witch. You and the kid can have water while we ready the horses."

"Emma," Maggie cried. "Let me—"

Gutierrez drew back his fist to quiet her. But before he swung, Brody and his men stepped out of hiding and surrounded them. In seconds, Brody had Emma off the ATV and in his arms, while the rest of his men kept their weapons trained on the two other guys.

"Back off," Gutierrez suddenly yelled as everyone's attention went to him. "Back off or I kill her."

Horrified, Colin watched as the deputy held Maggie like a shield in front of him. The man slid a huge knife up close to her throat. Everyone's attention had been diverted by Brody Ryan saving the baby himself, and now Maggie was in deep trouble. Unacceptable.

"Where can you go, Gutierrez?" Ethan called out loudly. "It's over. You're surrounded. Let her go."

"It's not over," the deputy answered as he dragged Maggie back a step. He sounded desperate—almost insane. "A man with more power than you can imagine is waiting for us. He will not accept losing. This witch woman is to be used as bait. *El Jefe* wishes to deal with the Anglo Fairfax himself, and he will kill me and anyone else who stands in the way."

Colin hadn't taken so much as a breath while he sighted the deputy's back through his scope. He cautioned himself not to let the words make him lose focus. His grip was loose. His trigger finger poised.

One good shot was all he needed. But Maggie was so close. He couldn't take the man down with a bullet to the back or head without running the risk of shooting Maggie, too.

Thankfully, Gutierrez made a monumental mistake just then. He tried to back up a few more feet, but his feet slipped on the sand and pebbles. Maggie twisted and jerked, trying to get away.

And Colin took advantage of the opportunity.

His shot hit the deputy in the shoulder, exactly as he'd planned. Gutierrez shrieked in pain, released his hold and dropped the knife, while Maggie took off running toward her father and Emma.

Ethan had his hands on Gutierrez in seconds. But the man was sniveling and crying and swearing he'd only done as he was ordered.

Colin took a couple of steps toward Maggie and saw her pull Emma into her arms. Then she spotted him and called out, "Colin. Thank the Lord you're all right." She held the baby in one arm and reached out with her other arm to invite Colin to join them.

He took another step toward them, but then hesitated. "You're okay?"

"We're fine. Come see for yourself."

He shook his head. "There's one more thing I need to do. You and Emma go to your father's house. Stay safe."

"Colin, you can't mean to go after the black witch." Maggie's voice cracked as she took a step in his direction. "He has power you don't understand. Let him go. The task force will get him. There's no need for you to—"

"He wants me. You and your family will all be in danger until I face him." Besides, he thought as he turned his back and headed in the direction of the line shack, he had a score to settle with this so-called *brujo*.

A reckoning for John.

Colin didn't think much of black magic anyway. After all, what could magic do against a rifle and very real bullets?

As Colin drew close to the line shack he could see up ahead, he listened for any sign of an assailant. Did a *brujo* attack in the same way as any other man?

Looking around, Colin noted that even the mesquite and sage nearby seemed to shiver with cold. All of nature silently screamed out its anxiety in the dead of night. Did something unnatural and ungodly lurk among the shadows in that stand of trees? Or was it more likely that the disturbance he felt was coming from the direction of the large rock outcropping behind his back?

Closing in on the shack, Colin snuck over the last

few meters and flattened himself against the rough-sawn wood wall. He didn't know if pure evil was waiting for him inside the lifeless-looking line shack, or just the man who had ordered John's murder.

Whichever, Colin was determined to best him. This was no suicide mission, despite what Maggie thought. Yes, he knew she believed him ready to die. But that was far from the case. He had not yet spent enough time touching her or kissing those soft, full lips. The mere sound of her voice in the dark earlier had reminded him of how badly he needed many more hours of holding her, of watching her while she slept. He would give up everything for decades more of drowning in those blazing green eyes.

He was not done with Maggie Ryan yet. Not by a long shot.

A complete stillness in the air reminded him of the current threat—of a man with a black hole for a soul, who wanted nothing more than Colin's destruction. This *brujo* would undoubtedly be a man of nature. A man who used nature to his own advantages. Outside was where this witch would want to make his stand.

But nothing stirred outside, so Colin's choice would be to meet this man inside. Reaching the shack's door, his hand eased out to wrap around the latch.

"Ah, Señor Fairfax. At last we meet." A brown-skinned man, slightly shorter but more muscular than he was, seemed to form out of thin air directly behind him.

Twisting, Colin could see in the starlight that this was a man used to being obeyed. But Colin felt confident he would be able to take him down. If all things were equal.

He raised the rifle and muttered, "You thought you

could kill me, but I guess you lose again. I'm here, *brujo*. Here and ready to see you reach justice."

"You are thinking that you will kill me before I kill you, *sí?*" In a move too quick to see with the human eye, the *brujo* snatched the rifle and flung it out into the night. "So, now you still believe you have an even chance?"

The drug lord laughed, and the sound of his laughter chilled the blood in Colin's veins. "Do not deceive yourself, Anglo dog. You have caused me too many problems. No one would have ever guessed the truth, until your nosy questions. Not even Governor Garcia knew his daughter had been killed with the traitor Juan. And my secret would have stayed that way forever. If not for you."

"You're a murdering thug and an imposter." Colin balanced on the balls of his feet, waiting for the man to make the first move. "You have no honor, not even for a thief. You deserve to die for your evil ways."

"You still cling to your hope for salvation?" The dark witch raised a fist and the sound of thunder blasted through the air.

Chuckling as Colin flinched, he said, "I do not play fair, gringo. That would be no fun—for me. You have caused me much trouble, and you must die. But before I kill you, I want you to look at what you leave behind." The drug lord waved his arm and the sound of rustling came from the bushes about thirty meters off to their left.

Colin shot a quick glance in that direction and saw Maggie coming through the brush with her brother. "Go back, Mags," he called out. "Let me handle this. Ethan, take her away from here."

"You are less than nothing, Fairfax." The drug lord narrowed his eyes. "Like garbage ready to toss. But the woman… I have an itch to visit South America, and she is my ticket out of the States. After that, perhaps she will make a pretty plaything. We shall see."

"Colin," Maggie called out as Ethan kept her from coming any closer. "Don't listen to him. Please let the authorities take care of bringing him in."

With his body strung tight from surging adrenaline, it was all Colin could do to keep his hands still. "This is between us, *brujo*. Leave her out of it. My brother deserves justice."

"Enough of the fun then, Anglo?" The drug lord chortled again. "Yes, I believe it is time." The entire night seemed to explode with the sound of the *brujo*'s evil laughter.

But the eruption of light and noise wasn't just coming from the witch devil's laughter. Out of the corner of his eye, Colin saw Seguro explode out of the darkness and race toward the *brujo*.

"Stay back!" Colin feared for the dog's life. "Maggie, call off the dog."

Snarling and barking, the devil dog halted a few feet away and seemed to be waiting for his chance.

"Too late," the *brujo* announced. "It is still your time to die, Fairfax. Nothing can save you. And then I will be free to do as I please with the woman."

By the time Colin looked back, the drug lord had his hand on the heavy gold chain around his neck. He lifted it in Colin's direction and grinned with evil intent.

"*Adios, amigo*," the *brujo* snickered.

Colin moved fast, without really understanding what he was doing. He thrust the heel of his hand upward, heading straight below the drug lord's chin with a move from the guerilla warfare tactics he'd practiced for so long it was now instinct.

But his quick movement accomplished more than Colin would have hoped. With heady velocity, his hand snapped right through the chain. Gold links scattered on the ground as the heel of Colin's hand continued to plow upward and onward, driving right into the drug lord's Adam's apple.

Without a sound, the Mexican *brujo* dropped to the ground in a limp heap. Colin didn't have a chance to check for a pulse, yet he knew that, one way or another, the *brujo* was out of commission. Just breaking his chain seemed to take the life right out of the evil man.

Seguro sniffed at the limp and lifeless body and then jumped and barked happily. Instantly, Maggie was upon Colin, wrapping her arms around his neck and her legs around his waist.

She cried and laughed and kissed him senseless. "I thought you were dead," she bubbled between the kisses. "How did you do that? How'd you beat the power of a *brujo?*"

Colin held her close and cherished her very much alive heartbeat, thudding in time with his own. "I have no idea what I did. I don't think it was me. Maybe it was a combination of heaven's justice for John—and mostly your protection charm—that saved us."

Maggie giggled and set off sweet bells ringing in his ears. "My little protection charm could never have outdone such strong black magic."

He gently touched her cheek. Then, placing his palms on either side of her face, he lasered a kiss across her full mouth. Her lips were warm and searching, rich with both passion and tenderness. He felt alive from the top of his head to the soles of his feet.

"It doesn't matter, my sweet witch," he said after lifting his head. "Nothing matters right now except you."

Maggie's *curandera* grandmother, Abuela Lupe, climbed her way up the narrow path of her mother's Vera Cruz mountainside. It was nearly dawn and she knew there wasn't much time left.

Out of breath and with her heart thudding, Lupe prayed for a miracle. Prayed for enough time to allow her mother to save her own soul and to also save her great-grandchildren's future at the same time.

Brody Ryan had done it. He had actually performed three good deeds. He'd used his political power to clear his oldest son's woman and save her boy from a life in the shadows. He'd used his money and influence to bring a sad little girl and her guardian safely together with his second son. And now he had saved a baby girl and had given his daughter a reason to live.

Without his knowing it, those deeds had been the price of Brody's salvation.

Over the last year of her life, Lupe's mother, Maria, had changed her *bruja* ways. Maria had promised to reverse the curse she'd placed on the Ryan family so many years ago *if*—and that was a big *if*—Brody Ryan could also mend his ways and find his heart.

Last night, Brody, Lupe's son-in-law, had come through with the third and final good deed. His love for his children shone clear and true.

Now, if only Maria had enough strength left to reverse her curse before she died. She'd been on her deathbed for days. And Lupe was positive her mother would not live to see the sunset today.

At last, winded and nearly dropping, Lupe rounded the last bend in the path and spotted her mother's cabin. Racing the last few yards into the house, she ran to her mother's bed.

Surrounded by nursemaids, neighbors and descendents, Maria Elena Ixtepan, the most feared black witch in Mexico, lay taking her last breaths. But when Lupe knelt and took her hand, her mother opened her eyelids. Blind and nearly deaf, the old woman knew immediately who was there and why.

"Mi'ja," Maria whispered. "It is done. I am done."

"Mother, please listen. Brody Ryan has completed his three good deeds. You must reverse your curse. There isn't much time."

"Shush, daughter. Days ago I foresaw the deed being done and reversed the curse, fearing that I might not survive to see it through to the end."

Maria's cracked and dry lips creaked up in a half smile. "You never really understood my full powers, *mi'ja*. My blackest strength has always been in the power to see the future."

"So it's over." Lupe breathed a sigh of relief. "Thank heaven. Now you may go with God."

Her mother's weak hand gripped hers more tightly than Lupe thought possible. "I will rest in peace, daughter. But you and yours may find trouble after I am gone. Have I never told you to be careful what you wish for?"

Confused, Lupe was about to ask what she meant. But at that moment, her mother slipped into a coma.

"I love you, Mother," Lupe whispered to deaf ears.

All that day Lupe sat and waited. Just before sunset,

her mother took her last breath. And at that very moment Maria's mountain was thrown into complete darkness. The black witch was finally dead.

Tomorrow the sun will shine once more, Lupe thought as tears filled her eyes. But she still wished she'd had the chance to ask about her mother's last remark.

Chapter 15

Maggie had often wondered what people meant when they made reference to women being multitaskers. As she slid the clean diaper under Emma's bottom, listened for the washing machine to finish running another load of clothes, talked to her father on the phone, and at the same time thought about what she would say to Colin when he arrived—she got a handle on this multitasking thing.

"Yes, Dad," she said as she balanced the phone between her shoulder and ear. "I expect Colin to be back later this afternoon. No, I haven't seen him in the last three weeks. You know that."

The international task force had whisked Colin away from the line shack on the night he'd overpowered the drug lord. They'd flown her lover directly out of the country to Mexico City before she'd even had a chance to show him how much she cared.

He'd said he loved her. She'd thought of nothing else for the last three weeks. But in fact, two people had said they loved her on that same day. And one of them was being especially irritating at the moment.

"I know you want to throw a barbecue to honor everyone who helped take down the drug lord and his men, but…" Maggie was forced take a breath then and listen to her father.

"I'd give you anything you want, baby girl," Brody said. "And it's clear what you want is Colin Fairfax. But we owe the hands a big celebration. I can't put it off much longer."

When he was done, she said, "Give the guy a break. Hold off for a couple more days."

Give her a break, too. She and Colin had lots of catching up to do.

But her father was right in one way. It was past time to thank the ranch hands who'd spent a long, frozen night racing through the far reaches of the Delgado rangeland on ATVs, running down the bad guys. If it hadn't been for their help—and her father's timely appearance—Maggie and Colin both might have ended up dead that night.

"Have you heard the results of the drug lord's autopsy, little girl?" Her father's comments brought her mind back to their conversation. "Do you know that the *brujo* dropped dead not due to Colin's blow but because he'd secretly taken his own life with poison? Colin did break the man's black magic, but he had nothing to do with killing him."

"Yes, Dad. I had heard that. But thanks for making sure I knew. I'll let Colin know, too."

"Then also tell him that Deputy Gutierrez has confessed to everything and will spend the rest of his life in a Texas jail. Our Sheriff Ochoa has promised to be much more careful when he hires his next deputy. He'd better, if he wants to keep his job."

Maggie hesitated a moment, then said what she'd been putting off. "I never thanked you for backing me up that night. I don't think I've ever been so grateful to see anyone in my life—even though I thought you'd promised to send men when I called, not get involved yourself. Um…thanks, Dad."

Her father chuckled. "You're welcome, sweetheart."

She sighed into the phone, so full of emotion the tears were about to fall. "And I want to make sure you understand that I love you. I always have, you know."

It took Maggie a few hours to finish the laundry. Funny, how one tiny baby could get stuff so dirty. She'd also spent what had seemed like hours scrubbing the kitchen until the counters and floor shined. She wanted everything perfect for Colin's arrival.

After feeling a little queasy this morning, Maggie had decided to grab a cracker and skip breakfast and lunch to work on chores instead. But now that Emma was down for her nap, Maggie thought she would grab a bite to eat before taking her shower and getting herself prettied up in time for Colin's arrival.

She could hardly wait. There was so much to say to him. It had been killing her to keep quiet over these last days, but she hadn't told him anything yet. In her opinion such important news shouldn't be shared long distance. His expression when she finally told him would be worth waiting for.

Opening up her refrigerator door, Maggie stood in

the artic blast of cold air and stared inside. What did she want to eat? Absently, she pulled the band from her hair and let the ponytail she always wore while cleaning go free. Milk and soda crackers? Nope. She was getting awfully tired of having that every morning. Something else. Something more satisfying….

"Hi." Colin's voice, coming from behind, startled her.

"Colin? You're…you're…early." Gasping, for a moment she just stared at his gorgeous face. "Thank God." She slammed the refrigerator door as she swung fully around to face him. "You're finally here."

"Yes." The look in his eyes was undecipherable. Was it anger? Desire? Hunger?

Maggie reveled in the thrill of standing this close to the man she loved. She wanted to soak him up. But the hungry wolf look in his eyes, never wavering for an instant from her face, sent a chill up her neck. She soon felt her own fierce demand enveloping her body as it trickled down her spine and landed in her belly.

Darn, why had he come back early? she wondered, wishing she'd had the opportunity to shower. "I thought you were going to stop to pick up your mother in San Antonio and bring her down here for a visit." Her words came out shaky, and her throat had gone dry.

"I'll go back later." The sound of his voice was rough, harsh.

"Well, do you want to talk it out first? Have you practiced what you'll say when you see her?"

"Later."

Maggie fiddled with her hair, lifted it off her neck and let the air conditioning dry her sweaty skin. "Well, then, I have something important to talk to you about. It's imperative that I tell you this before we do anything else. Do you want to sit down and I'll fix us a soda while I say what I have to say?"

"Later."

She saw his expression change from hunger to desperation and knew what it meant. "But…"

He took a step, plunged his fingers into her hair and tugged her to him. No time for words. He just plundered her mouth.

And she suddenly had no objections.

A new kind of need surged through her, then it spiked as she felt it surge in him as well. She thought she'd known his many moods, but this voracious appetite he'd brought to her today was different. Without releasing her mouth, he tore at her shirt until it disappeared, then tore at his own. Before she could catch her breath they were both naked, standing right in her kitchen in broad daylight.

And she didn't care a bit.

His mouth crushed hers with a demand for speed. Her head spun and her heart jumped in her chest as he lifted her up and deposited her on the sparkling clean counter. Still kissing her, their lips locked in rampant desire, he shoved her legs apart and moved between them.

And he entered her in one mighty thrust.

She gasped with the pure pleasure of having him inside her again. Her hands flailed wildly, grabbing for anything to hold on to, trying to steady herself. Steady her racing heart. Her fingers dug into his shoulders and his hands grabbed her hips as he hammered into her.

More, she thought vaguely. Locking her legs around his waist, she simply lost her mind. Hearing a crazy, primal drumbeat pounding inside her ears, she opened her eyelids and saw in Colin's eyes the same dark excitement that was pouring through her veins.

More. The fire leapt between them, snapping and popping and flaring. Wild with pure desperation now, she took everything he gave and still wanted more. Higher and higher they went, until, at last, a sudden explosion and waves of pleasure drove her dumb and blind.

But not deaf. His breath whooshed out from above her with one final push. And before the rolling thunder stopped inside her she felt it quaking through him.

Her mind was disjointed, splintered in a thousand pieces. Limp as a dishrag, she was pleased to note he trembled, too. She could feel his body rumbling inside hers.

But this had been all wrong, she thought, as her mind invaded her pleasure. She should've told him first. Though, somehow, at the moment, she couldn't bring herself to care.

"Ah," she managed after a couple of choppy breaths.

"Just wait." His voice was nothing more than a raw gasp. "I'll back up and help you off in a minute. Wait one more second…"

"It's okay. I'm fine like I am. I mean, I need a minute to get myself together, too."

Colin didn't know what to say, so he leaned a hand down on the counter and let his breathing ease back to normal. He'd thought about her every second for the last, very long three weeks. But it had never occurred to him how much he loved her. Not until this moment. What a hell of a way to come to the realization that he didn't want to take his next breath without her beside him. Savaging her probably wasn't considered the best way to say "I need you."

"Colin, I have to tell—"

"Wait a second. Let me explain myself." He finally took a step back and let her slide to the floor, feet first. "The last time I saw you, there in the clearing with Deputy Gutierrez wrapped around you like a chain, my heart stopped. They—the deputy and the drug lord— intended to hurt you. I'd never understood completely what it meant to be afraid before, but I wanted to kill them. Not for any reason noble or fair. Not even for revenge. I just wanted them to suffer."

"Oh, Colin." She looked at him with such devotion that he backed up a step.

"Look," he added, after taking another quick breath. "I know it wasn't my blow that killed that bastard *brujo*. But I wish it had been me that finished him. In the end, he got off easy."

Maggie's eyes narrowed. "Not if you believe as I do. To my way of thinking, he'll be spending eternity burning for his sins."

Not able to remain still, Colin stepped away from her and searched for his clothes.

He was revved up now and letting the rest of his fury and adrenaline roll out in a stream of words. "Damn that evil man to bloody hell! Let him burn. And damn myself for falling so much in love with you that I can't even think."

Maggie had never seen Colin in such a state. But-toning up, she watched while he stepped into his pants and drew the T-shirt over his head. "Colin, please sit down. Let's talk. I love you, and if you really do love me, things will all work out. I know it."

She pulled a couple bottles of water out of the

fridge and handed him one. Then she sat down at the
kitchen table, hoping he would calm down enough to
sit beside her.

Swallowing back a huge gulp of the cold liquid,
Maggie shivered as Colin took a slug of his own, then
he turned and began pacing the floor. She should be the
one pacing. There was so much to say.

Where to start? "Where do we go from here?" She'd
only asked the question rhetorically.

When he opened his mouth, she stopped him from
saying anything by holding her palm in the air. "No,
I didn't mean that literally—not yet. What I guess
I'm asking is, what do you see as a future for me…
and for Emma?"

Colin finally sat down and took her hand. "I'll have
to speak to my mother. The final word on her granddaughter should be hers. But if I have any say, you and
Emma will always be together. I couldn't separate you."

The breath wheezed right out of her lungs and her
shoulders slumped. One big hurdle down. If it was to
be woman to woman, Maggie had no fears. She and
Emma's grandmother were bound to come to a satis-
factory resolution. She was so grateful to Colin for
being reasonable and on her side that she nearly kissed
him. But she knew what would happen between them
if she did, and there was more to say. So much more.

Tightening her grip on his fingers, she looked
directly into his eyes and said, "My love, I found out a
couple of days ago that you and I are expecting our own
child." His eyes widened, then darkened as he stared at
her. "I waited to tell you until we could be together. I
guess…I guess I wanted to ask now what you see as a
future for all of us."

Colin dropped her hand like it had burned his fingers, then he stood and kicked back his chair with a loud scrape. "You lied to me? About the family curse? You lied."

Uh-oh. She'd gone about this wrong. Backward.

"No, listen," she begged, holding her arms out to him.

He shook his head violently. "What else have you lied about? About loving me? Damn you all to bloody hell." He glared at her. "I should've known not to trust anyone so different. It's my own stupid fault."

With that, he turned and stormed out of the house in a cloud of fury, leaving Maggie collapsed on the table in a heap of self-doubt, and having herself one hell of a pity party.

Chapter 16

After a hard two-hour drive, punctuated by every curse he'd ever learned—in several languages—Colin arrived at the residence motel where his mother was staying. Unbuckling his seat belt, he sat in the car for a few minutes just staring blankly out the windshield.

His throat hurt. The edges of his hands were bloody from pounding them on the steering wheel. What a fool he'd been.

And to top it off, he'd also been a rude twit.

The pained look on Maggie's face when he'd called her a liar would stick with him for the rest of his life. The woman he loved. How could he have said such a thing without thinking it through? All right, so he had been shocked. And hurt. More than a little hurt. Things between them had been so intense that he wasn't in his right mind. But that was no excuse.

He'd been thinking of how he would gladly give his life so that she wouldn't be hurt. And what had he done? Shot off his cheeky mouth and caused her pain.

Sighing, Colin rubbed at his temple. His thoughts were so muddled. He should have stayed put and heard her through. But the idea of becoming a father scared him senseless. He'd been barely coming to terms with the idea of loving a witch. It was too soon to think of the future. Too soon to visualize what came next.

But she'd taken that little problem neatly off his hands, hadn't she? He still wanted to know why she'd felt it necessary to trick him. She was a witch, after all. She could have simply bewitched him to get what she wanted.

Bugger it. Talk about shattered minds. When he'd first thought that about himself, he had no idea at all what it really meant to have shattered thoughts. None whatsoever.

Scraping at his glassy eyes, Colin locked the car and made his way to visit his mother—the other weird woman in his life.

"Colin, you're hurt. What's happened to make you so unhappy?" His mother took one look and dragged him inside her tiny suite of rooms.

"I'm not hurt," he lied. "Not a scratch on me. And don't you look well—smashing, actually." He hadn't seen her since his father's funeral, but she seemed ten years younger.

"Now, now," she said, and made a clucking sound. "Wash that bit of blood off your hands, love, then sit down. Sit there at the little table and I'll make you a nice cuppa while you tell me all about the dear girl you love, and what has made you both so miserable."

"What?" He would sit, but he was sure he'd never mentioned being in love. He'd only just come to that unfortunate realization himself.

"Your young woman's name is Maggie Ryan, isn't that right, *a stór?*" His mother took the whistling kettle from the stove and poured hot water over the tea to steep. "Lovely name, that. I had a great aunt they called Maggie. She might have been married to a Ryan, too, if I'm recalling the truth of it. But I believe your Maggie's true given names are Margarita Elena Inez Delgado. I suppose half Irish is better than none."

She gave him a wink. "Though, you've never thought so, have you, boyo?"

Colin wasn't ready to talk about his relationship with Maggie. Nor about the half-and-half status of his Irish blood. Particularly not with the woman to whom he hadn't even spoken in so many years he could barely remember. He squared his shoulders.

"Are you ready to meet your granddaughter?" he asked, hoping to take her mind off the other touchy subject. "I thought I'd take a room here for the night, and then we could motor to Zavala Springs in the morning."

"Yes. I suppose that would be nice. I want to meet your young woman face-to-face."

"And then I thought we might visit John's grave." He ignored her remarks and refused to let her keep circling around to Maggie. "Pay our respects there. His grave marker hasn't been remade just yet. But I have ordered the work done."

His mother's face clouded over at the mention of John. "A mother is not supposed to stand at the graveside of her child. Once I feared…I thought your grave would be the one I might be seeing, not John's." She closed her eyes, and he watched her straightening her spine and working through the difficult emotions.

Pouring the tea, she glanced over finally with a sly half smile. "Do not distract me from the real question, *a stór*. Your feelings for this young woman—whom you love, don't deny it—are making you unhappy. I want to know why."

"Stop calling me your 'treasure.' I'm not." Colin's fury bubbled over, and he couldn't hide his anger anymore. "I haven't been anything to you ever since you left and walked away.

"If you want the truth," he continued, without letting her respond to that statement. "Maggie is too much like you. She's…uh…odd. No, check that. She's a bloody witch, with a Texas accent instead of Celtic. We come from two entirely different worlds."

On a rant now, he stood and paced the small open room. "And that kind of relationship worked out so well for you and my father, didn't it? Maggie would never fit in with life in England. And eventually she would stop loving me and leave. Just like you did."

His shoulders slumped. "I couldn't take that. I'd end up like Father, all shriveled up and dying from the loneliness."

"Oh, Colin. You've never known? The man never told you the truth? I thought… I thought… Well, now I see."

He stopped walking and stared at her. Waiting. Holding his breath and waiting.

His mother stood, too. She went to the sink, then turned. "Through the years," she said slowly, taking her time, "I never stopped loving either you or your father. He *sent* me away. I didn't leave you both, not willingly."

Sighing, she fiddled with the faucet. "When my mother came to England to help with John's illness, your father's attitude toward me began changing. His own mother was badgering him then about the difference in our backgrounds. She nagged and whined and went on about how his being married to an Irish witch would ruin his career chances, and the family's name.

"I was helpless," she added, as her voice cracked. "My youngest son lay on death's door. My mother had the cure. What could I do? I thought my love for your father…for all of you, should be enough to see us through. 'Twasn't. Not nearly."

Wiping her eyes with a paper towel, she sniffed and went on, "In the end, he gave me no choice. 'Take the sick boy and leave the healthy one,' he'd said. 'But go and never come back.'"

Collin's heart stopped and he couldn't believe what he was hearing. "Go on," he said in a strangled voice.

"If your father died shriveled and lonely, 'twas his own bad nature that made him that way." His mother fisted her hand and brought it down on the counter. "I begged, pleaded, to be allowed to see you. To have you come for school and live with me and John. But your father wouldn't hear of it."

She opened her hand, palm up, begging Colin now to understand—to believe. "Even with all of that, my love for your father never wavered. I tried to kill it. *He* tried to kill it. Still, it never died. That was my burden. But I don't love what he did to you." She looked up at him, and Colin saw the steel in her eyes behind the sheen of tears. "I hate what his lies have done."

Taking a ragged breath, she bit her lip and came closer. "I should've known. When you stopped trying to reach me, stopped calling and writing. I should've tried harder. Gotten around him somehow. That's my fault, *a stór*." She placed tender fingertips against his cheek. "Forgive me."

Stunned, Colin stood frozen to the spot. But in moments, the warmth of her hand began thawing the artic ice that had encased his heart for too many years.

"Mother." He fell into her arms, hugged her so tightly he worried about her bones breaking.

"I love you, son," she whispered. "And you love your darlin' Irish-Mexican witch. I know it will take time to forgive me, but don't let your father ruin your entire life. He's gone. Find a way to your own happiness and then never let it go. Real love is magic."

The word made him think, so Colin reared back— but he didn't let her loose. "Speaking of magic, have you been…uh…dabbling in my life? Watching out for me?"

"No. Why are you asking? What has happened?"

"A couple of things. In particular, I somehow broke a *brujo*'s black magic. Just sliced my hand right through his golden chain of evil like it was butter. Now, how do you suppose I did that?"

She laughed, and the sound of it seemed to brighten up the room. "Oh, darlin' boy, it's coming through. Think of it! The magic that was my mother's, her family's heritage for generations, has settled in you.

"John always wished he'd been born to it," she added more quietly. "But it never came to him. Maybe giving your heart to a witch was what brought out the quirk in your genes."

Chuckling, she kissed his cheek. "Methinks you doth protest the differences between you too roundly, *a stór*.

Maybe you should take a good look at who you are, before you refer to anyone else as 'different.'"

Colin wasn't sure what to do with all his new knowledge—these new emotions. He wasn't even sure who he was anymore. Maybe all he needed was a little rest, in order to see things more clearly. But that would have to wait, he decided, as he drove the rental, with his mother and all her luggage, down the main street of Zavala Springs.

He and his mother had spent most of the night talking, crying, holding on to one another. He'd soothed her when she finally dissolved into full-blown hysterics over John's death. She'd soothed him, even rocked him as one would a little child, when he threw a tantrum over their lost years and his father's deception.

He told her everything about Maggie and Emma and the fascinating Delgado Ranch. It was quite possible he had never said so much at any one time before in his life. But the one thing he'd left unsaid, the fact that he would soon be a father himself, was Maggie's secret to tell.

Still not sure why she'd felt it necessary to feed him an elaborate story about a family curse, he knew that it simply didn't matter anymore. If she'd wanted her own child so badly, he would've been glad to oblige her anyway. Making love to her, having a future in front of him, had changed his life in ways he hadn't even considered.

Yawning, he turned down Maggie's street and immediately felt wide awake. Would she ever forgive him for being such a jerk? Did she love him enough to put up with his selfish ways and big mouth?

"Who are all those people, *a stór?*" His mother

looked confused as she studied the small crowd gathering in Maggie's driveway.

He saw, but didn't understand the significance. "They're Maggie's family. Her two brothers, their wives and children. I wonder why they've come?"

"If you're asking me," his mother began with a smile, "it feels like a party. And more than that, they seem to know we're on the way. I can feel the welcome in them, even from this distance."

Having his mother spouting mystical things like that would have bothered him once upon a time, but now he only wondered if he could learn to feel it, too. "They're a great family, Mother. I know you'll love them as much as they'll love you."

He parked behind the others, got out, and then introduced everyone around. The women hugged. Maggie's brothers kissed his mother's cheeks and shook his hand.

"We need to take the kids and Mrs. Fairfax inside, out of the wind, because it's actually getting colder this morning. Typical change of weather in South Texas," Blythe told them. "Why don't you men bring the food and drinks into the kitchen?"

His mother grinned, shimmering all over in the glow of goodwill, with her arms around the two little ones. "Grand idea. Colin, would you be bringing my things inside?"

"I'm not sure we'll be staying, Mother."

She patted his shoulder. "Yes, of course you are. And I'll be thanking you for the overnight bag first, please."

He shrugged and retrieved her bags as the women disappeared inside. When he moved to go inside, too, both of Maggie's brothers were laying in wait for him before he reached the back step.

Ethan smacked him on the back. "Well, old man, how does it feel? Being a first-time father is bound to be a bit different for you. Josh and I have had a lot practice. I mean, you've taken care of Emma, but a newborn…" He made a face then and chuckled under his breath. "Hmm, actually, I guess that'll be a different sort of experience for all of us."

"Maggie told you? About the baby coming?"

Josh laughed and shook his head. "No. No need. We're all pretty much in the same situation."

"What are you saying?" Colin was dumbfounded and knew he must look the fool. "You two are both having babies, too? The whole family at once? What a gigantic coincidence that is."

"Not at all," Josh said with a knowing nod to his brother. "We've been living under a family curse for the last fifteen years. I'm sure Maggie must have told you. That's why none of us was…uh…careful. So when our great-grandmother quietly lifted her curse before she died, none of us was prepared. We didn't know to…er…"

"Change our ways," Ethan finished for his brother with a grin. "Not until Abuela called us. But by then it was too late. We figured you and Maggie weren't being…careful…either. So, congratulations, 'Dad.' We're all here today to help the ladies celebrate giving up beer and coffee for the next nine months."

"Then…she…" Oh, what a blithering idiot he'd been. Maggie hadn't been telling him stories after all.

"Kinda leaves you speechless, doesn't it?" Josh laughed as he made his way inside carrying the heavy ice chest.

Colin was the last through the door, burdened down with his mother's luggage. He searched the crowded kitchen for Maggie, but didn't find her. He had a lot of groveling to do.

His mother finally stopped him as he eased through the crowd. "Your sweetheart has taken herself up to the attic to make up the room." His mother held Emma in her arms and didn't look as though she would ever give the baby up. "Maggie says I'll be comfortable there, as it's a light, airy space. I'm sure she'll take as good care of me as she has done with my granddaughter."

Smiling at his mother's words, Colin reached to gently stroke Emma's cheek.

"She's the welcoming girl I knew she would be, son. You chose well. You should be happy with yourself."

He hadn't chosen a thing. This had all simply happened around him. But he would be happy in the end, if only Maggie still loved him enough to forgive him.

"Well, go on," his mother urged. "I plan on staying right here with Emma. Take my things up. Face your future."

Maybe he should have written down everything he needed to say. Made a list of his good and bad points, so Maggie could clearly see what she was in for.

But the minute he walked into the attic bedroom and saw her bending over to make up the bed, he concluded all of that would wait for another time. His mind was simply not up to the strain right now. Not when she was this close.

He dropped the luggage and cleared his throat to let her know he was there. She jumped, her surprised yelp admirable. Good set of lungs, he thought.

Gasping and holding her fist to her heart, she said, "Colin, you scared me half to death. Don't do that. You'll turn my hair gray."

He pursed his lips to keep the broad grin off his face. "You'd be beautiful with gray hair. In fact, you *will* be beautiful with gray someday. It'll probably be the color of silver, and sexy as hell. I can't wait."

He'd expected at least a small smile, but she stood there with a sober expression and just studied him. Her green eyes blazed with heat, and he felt his body go tense.

"I have a lot to say," he managed past a suddenly dry throat. "Apologies. Begging for forgiveness…" The words dried up now, too, and he felt a new kind of terror.

She must have taken pity on him, because she closed the gap between them, reached out and grabbed the front of his shirt. "Show me."

She needn't ask twice. In a blink, his lips were on hers. His hands ran frantically over her body, closed over her breasts. She moaned and leaned into him. And he thought of how easy it would be to stand here doing this—silently touching her and tasting her—for eternity.

However, the most important words refused to be silenced. "I love you so much. And if you want me, I won't ever walk out again. You'll have to kick me out of this house to be rid of me."

Maggie heard herself moan as she reared back in shock. "You're staying? Not going back to London?"

Something big had changed in him. She would figure out what it was eventually. But for right now, lust was crawling up her spine and making her a bit stupid. The intensity of his kiss brought her a sweet ache of belonging. This was where she'd longed to be. With the man who loved her just as she was. This was her real home. Here. In his arms.

She tried to take a breath, decided it wasn't strictly necessary, and went back to kissing him. "I love you," she whispered against his lips. "You can stay. Please stay. And please keep telling me you love me."

"Every day." He rubbed up and down her arms, and she could feel a monster hunger building higher in him, too.

But he stepped back. "Today will be long, and I have something else to say. When do you suppose we can…get rid of everyone and be alone?"

"Say?" She laughed out loud as her heart seemed to fly. "I know better. Talking isn't what's on your mind, Colin Fairfax. It's not what's on mine, either." She sighed heavily. "But you're right. For now, we'll have to put off ravaging each other until much later. Just think of what a great night we'll have when we're finally alone."

"No, actually," he argued, "I do have something to say."

She shoved at his chest and giggled. "Come on, big guy. For heaven's sake, if you really have something to say, just get it off your chest now and be done with it."

He looked down at his feet. "I was hoping to have the lights dimmed."

"So I couldn't see your face? Colin, be a man. You can say anything to me."

With an unhappy grunt, he reached into his pocket, pulled out a velvet box and shoved it at her. "Fine. Then how's this for romantic in broad daylight?"

Plopping down on the bed in complete shock, she opened the box and gaped. "Is this what I think?"

"I didn't imagine you'd be interested in a standard diamond. But I would've found one anyway, if Mother hadn't given me this last night. It was her mother's wedding ring. The emeralds remind me of your eyes." His voice faltered. "If you hate it, we can go shopping—"

"Then you mean this as an engagement ring?" She suddenly felt numb all over.

Colin bent to one knee and took her hand. "Marry me, Maggie Ryan. Add my name to your long list of names. Have my child and then we'll work on having more. I want four."

He gazed into her eyes. "Grow old and gray with me, Mags, and I'll never stop telling you how much I love you."

She'd thought her heart had been full, knowing children were coming at last to the Ryan family. But there was space left in her heart for this wonderful man. A lot of space.

"Can we have six kids?" she whispered through growing tears. "That's how many I've always dreamed of having."

He sighed heavily, took the ring from the box and put it on her finger. "Maggie, my love, you can have anything your heart desires. I could never deny you anything."

Her breath hitched on a sob as she leaned over to place her lips against his. In the next instant, the kiss went deeper and passion flamed, the driving heat scorching them both. Maggie figured it would always be this way. She hoped so.

Somewhere in the back of her mind, she also sincerely hoped her family was talking among themselves downstairs, because she sure had a lot more to say right here.

More to say with her lips. With her body. With her whole heart.

Epilogue

"That's it," Maggie said, as she looked up into the blazing blue eyes of the man she loved, sitting at her bedside. "One baby plus Emma will have to do. I'm not going through that again."

The whole hospital room full of family laughed. But she'd meant every word.

"You'll feel differently soon enough *a gra*, my child." Her mother-in-law stroked her hair and smiled down on her over Colin's shoulder. "I said the same at first, but changed my mind within days."

Maggie rolled her eyes, then quickly caught sight of the beautiful baby boy being passed around the crowd. "He really is something special, isn't he?"

Colin retrieved his son and placed him in her arms. "He's gorgeous. Looks just like his mum."

"No, I think he looks a lot like your mother."

Maggie's chest swelled, so stuffed full of love she didn't think she'd ever get over this unique feeling. "Maybe we could have just one more. A girl, to be a playmate for Emma, would be nice. I always wanted a baby sister when I was little."

"Emma's going to have lots of playmates," Maggie's father told her from the far side of the room. He was holding the two-week-old daughter of Josh and Clare in one arm, the ten-day-old daughter of Ethan and Blythe in the other, and looking every bit the proud grandpa he was.

Ah, just look down from heaven at this now, Elena darlin'. Brody Ryan's thoughts went back to the beginning. Back to when he'd first married and promised his loving wife they would have a big family, with tons of kids and grandkids. For too long he'd figured he had failed her. Now he felt redeemed. Whole again. His heart was bursting with gratitude for the second chance.

There you go, my lost love. All is finally as it should be, and I wish you could be here to see it.

Colin slid into the bed beside Maggie, gathered her and the baby up in his arms and rested his chin on her head. "The number is totally up to you, love, but give me a couple of years to recuperate from this ordeal first, will you?"

That earned him a room full of guffaws, but he wasn't done speaking his mind. "And," he added with a dramatic wave of his hand, "let's wait and see how much of a witch this one turns into." Colin still hadn't come to terms with his own magic, but he was slowly accepting the truth, and Maggie and his mother were helping him learn to use it.

At his mention of the baby perhaps becoming a witch,

too, they all laughed again. The sound of their laughter echoed down the halls and reverberated across the miles, straight to a verdant, lush mountainside in Vera Cruz.

Abuela Lupe listened, heard the happy, vibrating sound, and laughed herself. This was the way things were meant to be. Having happy celebrations of new life and true love.

After all, everyone knew love was the real magic.

* * * * *

Celebrate 60 years of pure reading pleasure with Harlequin®!

Step back in time and enjoy a sneak preview of an exciting anthology from Harlequin® Historical with THE DIAMONDS OF WELBOURNE MANOR

This compelling anthology features three stories about the outrageous Fitzmanning sisters. Meet Annalise, who is never at a loss for words… But that can change with an unexpected encounter in the forest.

Available May 2009 from Harlequin® Historical.

"I'm the illegitimate daughter of notoriously scandalous parents, Mr. Milford. Candidates for my hand are unlikely to be lining up at the gates."

"Don't be so quick to discount your charms, my dear. Or the charm of your substantial dowry. Or even your brothers' influence. There are as many reasons to marry as there are marriages."

Annalise snorted. "Oh, yes. Perhaps I shall marry for dynastic reasons, or perhaps for property or influence. After all, a loveless, practical marriage worked out so well for my mother."

"Well, you've routed me on that one. I can think of no suitable rejoinder." Ned rose to his feet and extended his hand. "And since that is the case, let me be the first to wish you a long and happy spinsterhood."

Her mouth gaped open. And then she laughed.

And he froze.

This was the first time, Ned realized. The first time he'd seen her eyes light up and her mouth curl. The first time he'd witnessed her features melded together in glorious accord to produce exquisite beauty.

Unbelievable what a change came over her face. Unheard of what effect her throaty, rasping laughter had on his body. It pounded a beat upon his ear, quickly taken up by his pulse. It echoed through him, finally residing in his stirring nether regions.

So easily she did it, awakened these sensations within him—without any apparent effort at all. And she had called him potentially dangerous? Clearly the intelligent thing for him to do would be to steer clear, to leave her to the tender ministrations of Lord Peter Blackthorne.

"You were right." She smiled up at him as she took his hand and climbed to her feet. "I do feel better."

Ah, well. When had he ever chosen the intelligent path?

He did not relinquish her hand. He used it to pull her in, close enough that he could feel the warmth of her. "At the risk of repeating Lord Peter's mistake and anticipating too much—may I ask if you'll be my partner in battledore tomorrow?"

Her smiled dimmed. Her breath came a little faster. His own had gone shallow, as if he'd just run a race—and lost. He ran his gaze over the appealing lift of her brow and the curious angle of her chin. His index finger twitched.

"I should like that," she said.

His finger trembled again and he lifted it, traced the pink and tender shell of her ear, the unique sweep of her jaw. Her pulse leaped beneath her skin, triggering his own. Slowly he tilted her chin up, waiting for her to object, to step back, to slap his hand away.

She did none of those eminently sensible things. Which left him free to do the entirely impractical thing.

Baby soft, the skin of her lips. Her whole body trembled when he touched her there.

He leaned in. Her eyes closed, even as she stood straight against him, strung as tight as a bow. He pressed his mouth to hers. It was a soft kiss, sweet and chaste. And yet he was hot and hard and as ready as he'd ever been in his life.

She drew back a little. Sighed. Their breath mingled a moment before she slowly backed away.

"Oh," she breathed. Her dark eyes were full of wonder and something that looked like fear. He took a step toward her, but she only shook her head. His out-stretched hand fell to his side as she turned to disappear into the wood. This was the first time, Ned realized. The first time, since he'd come to the house party at Welbourne Manor, that he'd seen her eyes light up.

* * * * *

*Follow Ned and Annalise's story in May 2009 in
THE DIAMONDS OF WELBOURNE MANOR
Available May 2009 from Harlequin® Historical*

*Available in the series romance section, or in the
historical romance section, wherever books are sold*

**We'll be spotlighting a different series
every month throughout 2009
to celebrate our 60th anniversary.**

Look for Harlequin® Historical in May!

**60 years of Harlequin,
600 years of romance
in Harlequin Historical!**

www.eHarlequin.com

HHBPA09

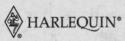

HARLEQUIN®

American ★ Romance®

LAURA MARIE ALTOM
The Marine's Babies

Men Made in America

Captain Jace Monroe is everything a Marine
should be—strong, brave and honorable. He's also
an instant father of twin baby girls he never knew
existed! Life gets even more complicated when he
finds himself attracted to Emma Stewart, his new
nanny. But can this sexy, fun-loving bachelor do
the right thing and become a family man?
Emma and the babies are counting on it!

Available in May
wherever books are sold.

LOVE, HOME & HAPPINESS

The Inside Romance newsletter has a NEW look for the new year!

Same great content, brand-new look!

The Inside Romance newsletter is a FREE quarterly newsletter highlighting our upcoming series releases and promotions!

Click on the Inside Romance link on the front page of
www.eHarlequin.com or e-mail us at
insideromance@harlequin.ca to sign up
to receive your FREE newsletter today!

You can also subscribe by writing to us at: HARLEQUIN BOOKS
Attention: Customer Service Department
P.O. Box 9057, Buffalo, NY 14269-9057

Please allow 4-6 weeks for delivery of the first issue by mail.

IRNNEW09

REQUEST YOUR FREE BOOKS!

2 FREE NOVELS PLUS 2 FREE GIFTS!

Silhouette® Romantic

SUSPENSE

Sparked by Danger, Fueled by Passion!

Silhouette®

Romantic

SUSPENSE

COMING NEXT MONTH

Available April 28, 2009

#1559 LADY KILLER—Kathleen Creighton
The Taken
When Tony Whitehall is enlisted to find out more about
Brooke Fallon Grant, who's accused of murdering her abusive ex-husband,
she insists that she—and her pet cougar, Lady—are
innocent. Sparks fly between Tony and Brooke as they try to save
the animal's life and discover who the killer really is.

#1560 HIS 7-DAY FIANCÉE—Gail Barrett
Love in 60 Seconds
Starting a new life in Las Vegas, Amanda Patterson never predicted she'd
be assaulted by a gunman in a casino. Owner Luke Montgomery fears bad
publicity and convinces her to keep quiet. When someone tries to kidnap
her daughter, Amanda agrees to Luke's plan to temporarily move in with
him and act as his fiancée, but their growing attraction soon puts them all
in danger.

#1561 NIGHT RESCUER—Cindy Dees
H.O.T. Watch
Wracked with survivor's guilt, former Special Forces agent
John Hollister agrees to put his suicide on hold to deliver medical
researcher Melina Montez to the mountains of Peru. As sexual heat and
desire flare, she reveals the fatal mission she's on to rescue her family,
and together they challenge each other to fight to stay alive for love.

#1562 HIGH-STAKES HOMECOMING—Suzanne McMinn
Haven
Intending to lay claim to his inherited family farm, Penn Ramsey is
shocked to discover the woman who once broke his heart. Willa also
claims the farm is hers, and when a storm strands them at the house
together, they discover their attraction hasn't died and all isn't as it seems.
Is the house trying to keep them from leaving? Or is something—or
someone—else at work here?

SRSCNMBPA0409